BEGAVAD

Love
Power
and
Royalty

The Beginning

First paperback edition December 2022

Book design by The Branding X and Milah M. Malaj

ISBN 978-1-7386990-0-1 (paperback)
ISBN 978-1-7386990-1-8 (ebook)

BOOK ONE: The Beginning

BOOK TWO: The Martian Alliance

BOOK THREE: The Reunion

BOOK FOUR: The Legacy

BOOK FIVE: The New Age

Thank you

Thank you to my mom for passing on the gift of writing and creativity, supporting and encouraging my dreams

Thank you to my ninja uncle for introducing me to the wonder and inspiring me

Thank you to my dad for encouraging me and my dreams

Thank you to my friends Keziah, Keziah, Karolina and Gia for the continuous support and excitement

Thank you to my art hippies and chicken buddies

Thank you to all my family and friends for all the support, encouragement and inspiration that you knowingly — and unknowingly — provided

And last but not least, thank you to my aunt Tenisha who from the very beginning has been the biggest supporter of my book and the fantasy world I created. Your excitement and belief is what kept me dreaming and is the reason why you are reading the words in this book. Without you, *all* of you, this fantasy of mine would have never come true and for that

I Thank You

Table of Contents

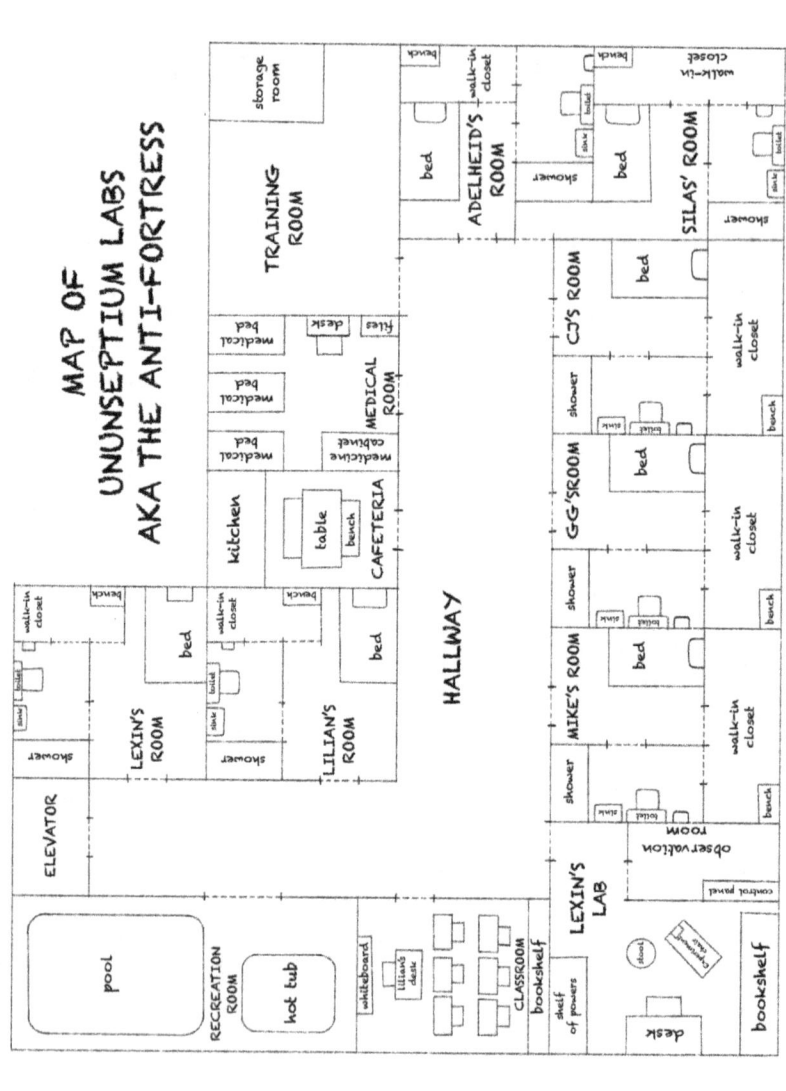

MAP OF
UNUNSEPTIUM LABS
AKA THE ANTI-FORTRESS

CHAPTER ONE

In the beginning, there was only God. But after seven days, he created the earth, and for a while, it was good. Until He created man, and they sinned. Many know the story of Genesis, where Adam and Eve were cast out of the Garden of Eden after being tempted by a former angel of heaven. It was a simpler time then. A world with only Humans, until the evil spirit that had been the first to tempt humankind, devised a new form of sin to plague the Humans with. The evil spirit created a tree flourishing with temptation and spread this doom to five different regions of the earth. These trees, similar to the one in the garden, gave not just the power of omniscience but the power to bend the distinct binding of the earth to thou's own will. Anyone who touched the tree would acquire the ability to possess and become the elements of fire, water, earth and air as well as the power of telepathy that would grant them access to anyone and everyone's mind born of the earth.

The first person to encounter the tree was a woman by the name of Harkolin. She resided in the land of Egypt. The other four who met the tree were from different tribes and spoke different languages from each other, as their encounter with the giving tree took place after the uprising of the Tower of Babylon. When they touched the tree, they consumed its power, and the evil spirit spoke to them and told them his intentions, which was to use them as vessels to wreak havoc on the Humans. Drawn in by the anomalous and captivating tree of temptation, they laid their hands on its bark, but with the fear of God deep inside them, they rebuked its power upon hearing its demands. God saw this and allowed them to keep their new abilities and use them for good. Harkolin and the others swore to this and thus created the Begavad society. Within a month of receiving their powers, the five Begavads came together in Egypt, where Harkolin readily greeted them in her home. As their languages were foreign, they quickly learned each other's tongues so that they could efficiently communicate. The night they had all finally learned to do so, they were sitting around a fire like the five individuals did each night, but this night was different. For this night was the night they established an unbreakable bond.

"We are... how doth thou say... begavad," Klorkem exclaimed. The others had looked at him confused, but Harkolin, their appointed leader, understood what he meant.

"He means to say that we are gifted," she said. Klorkem nodded, and the rest did as well, in pride and agreement. It was Klorkem who had inspired the name for the Begavad and it was he who suggested they keep their community exclusive. But Harkolin feared that their betrayal of the evil spirit who gave them this power would mean that the things he had promised would not last forever. She worried that the immortality promised to them with their abilities would run out. So, she suggested growing their kind. As the others fully trusted Harkolin, they followed suit. They soon realized that Harkolin was right, in a way, as their immortality was not hereditary and had to be passed on from parent to kin through a special ritual. So it became custom for the father of every family to give up their life to their child. They also realized that not all Begavads were born with the telepathic ability or all four elements. As time went on, they began to see Begavads displaying different abilities.

We created a hierarchy. Humans were at the bottom. Then there were advantageously mutated specimens: Humans who had mutated into a more genetically diverse being on their own and throughout evolution, separate from the Begavads. Then there were Elementes, a type of Begavad that possessed one element. There was a particular type of Elemente who possessed more power than regular Elementes. For example, Elementes with the water element could also become and manipulate ice. As well as a special breed of air Elementes who could manipulate the weather. After Elementes were Pentaelkays, they possessed two elements. Finally at the top of the hierarchy were the Alpha Begavad. They were direct descendants of the very first five Begavads created, and they possessed all four elements. As Alpha Begavad's we were always the ruler, queen, king or captain of our division, council or team because we were the highest form of being on earth. However, we never ruled over Humans, only our own kind. In the first few years of our existence, we lived amongst the Humans but after a while, they strayed further from the righteous path and revolted against the Begavad. So we segregated ourselves from the Humans and adapted to a life underground. We formed our new society away from Humans in environments where they could not survive, like the arctic, underwater and in the desert. As the human population grew throughout the years, we relocated to the least populated regions of the earth. Now we have five divisions of Begavad and five royal families amongst the Begavad society. There's the Harks who resided in the depths of Niagara Falls as the North American division. The Lambois were located in the Falkland Islands and made up the South American division. The Timpanis resided underneath the savannah as the African division. The Keyanis, the Asian division located in Maldive and the VonFriedls, the European division disguised in the Holy See of Rome. Their rulers were Harkolin Hark, Ishmael Lambois, Zazo Timpani, Mujerki Keyani, and Klorkem VonFriedl. They set the criteria for the perfect Begavad, but generations of Begavad later, something changed. Our values, morals and history were altered. We continued to segregate ourselves from Humans, only interjecting discreetly when most appropriate. These are the stories we are told as children of how we came to be and our purpose on Earth. But in the past billion years, our society has changed, and I no longer know what to believe. So, I have to make a choice. I have to understand how it all started and when things went wrong, so I can prosecute the guilty and change earth's fate and the fate of my people.

Adelheid Hark

Today is the first day of school, and this year I'm a senior in grade eleven. I spent my summer enthralled in the pages of my book that I had just finished writing. I was on my way to becoming a best-selling author. I had hoped that I could maybe afford a car once that happened. That way, I wouldn't have to take the city bus and be pestered by random people every day on my way to school, as I was today. In my opinion, if the bus isn't full, it's just implied that you should never sit right next to any stranger, but apparently, that is just *my* opinion. As the bus made its third stop, a boy came and sat right next to me, when there were three perfectly free seats to my left. He attempted to stir up a conversation, and I answered his questions reluctantly. Then I became irritated and impolitely made this clear.

"I'm sorry, who are you and why are you talking to me?"

"Hey, hey, calm down. I'm just a cool guy making conversation with a cute girl," he said. My eyes widened in shock as he spoke with such directness.

"No, you are a strange person talking to me, and I… this is my stop anyway, so I have to go," I said as I rushed off the bus. It really was my stop. As I walked down the street, I turned my head to see him running toward me. I looked forward and began to walk faster. He caught up to me in a second and tapped me on the shoulder. I immediately jerked my shoulder away and stopped. "Um, excuse me, boundaries, dude!" I huffed as I crossed my arms. I looked at the boy up and down. Though I had just snapped at him, he continued to walk beside me with a calm smile on his face. "So, what are you stalking me now?" He laughed and then shook his head.

"No, why would you say that?" He asked, shockingly. I began to explain to him that it was very unusual for people on the bus to start conversations with me, especially in the morning when most people are still tired and not in the mood to talk. I also told him that it was even more unusual when that same person attempts to follow you even after you've made it clear that you're not interested in being their friend. "I'm going to school," he said as he pointed down the street to my school.

"No way. You are going to my school?" I asked. He nodded and smiled.

"I'm not following you, I mean I am, but I'm not. I saw you wearing the school spirit wear and thought I'd get a head start on making friends," he said. I looked up at him and then smiled cautiously. We continued to walk down the street side by side. He was tall, almost six feet, it seemed. He was a light-skinned boy, only a few shades lighter than me. He had long, loose, spiralling, dark brown curls that bounced up and down on his head, falling close to his ears. His eyes were the most beautiful combination of blue and green that I had never seen before on a Black person.

"So you're new, I assume. I've never seen you around," I said. The stranger nodded and smiled. "And how do I know you're not just following me around to kill me later?"

"Trust me, if I wanted to kill you, I would have done it already," he said. I looked at him suspiciously. What an odd thing to say to someone you've just met.

"So, what's your name?" He asked.

"I am called Adelaide, of the Adelaides," I said. He looked at me with shock and then smiled and giggled.

"Well, I'm Silas, of the Silas'," he said mockingly. I looked at him perplexed.

"That's so weird. One of the characters in the book I wrote

is named Silas, but that's none of your business because you're a random stranger, and I don't even know why I'm entertaining you."

"Well, it's a very common name."

"No, it is not," I said, shaking my head. I felt it odd that his name was Silas and that he fit a similar description of the character from my book, but I figured it was just a coincidence. "So, where did you come from?" I asked as we finally got to the school. He jumped ahead to open the door with a smile, and I returned his smile as I walked in.

"Well, if you want to know more about me, then perhaps you should give me your number?" He asked confidently. I laughed and turned away. Conveniently, my friends were waiting for me in the cafeteria. I turned back to him with a stern smile.

"Ya, I'm not giving some guy who I don't even know my number. I'll give you my socials, though."

"I don't have any socials," he said.

"Really?" I asked. He shrugged.

"Well, if you actually go here, I'll need proof. A timetable with your name on it," I said as I backed away. "And then maybe, I'll consider giving you my number."

I walked up to my friends and watched him smirk as he went toward the main office.

"Girl, who is that? He's cute," May asked.

"Some guy I met on the bus... claims he goes here," I said.

Half the day went on and I continued to keep an eye out for Silas. Finally, it was lunchtime, but instead of going to the cafeteria to eat and socialize, I went to the music room. It appeared empty just the way I liked it. There was only the faint sound of the piano which I assumed was the radio. It wasn't until I approached the back of the music room that I noticed Silas sitting there. He smiled at me and continued playing his tune, which I recognized as Bach's "Prelude in C Major." I went over to the piano and stood beside it, facing him, resting my arm on the top.

"There are these silly theories that Bach was this half-human, half-immortal man that wrote songs to ward off evil spirits. I would believe them if it weren't for the fact that Bach is dead. If he was immortal, why isn't he still with us?" I asked. Silas nodded and then stopped playing.

"Do you play?" He asked.

"I do," I said as I sat down next to him on the piano bench. The warm room made me realize how cold his skin was as our arms brushed against each other.

"You're freezing. What are you a vampire?" He laughed and shook his head.

"Not exactly. I'm cold, but I'm not undead," he said. "That Bach theory though, think about it like this: what is being immortal? Do you define it as someone who can live forever or someone who actually does?" To me, those are the same things, but I just shrugged my shoulders because I wanted to know what he thought.

"Imagine, I'm immortal. I live for hundreds of thousands of years, and then I go to war, and I am blown to pieces. Obviously, I'm dead. Pieces of me scattered across the battlefield. The type of situation where Humpty Dumpty cannot be put back together again, but before that, I would have lived forever had I not gone to war. So am I still immortal?" He asked.

"Is that something that happened to you recently?" I joked. We both laughed, and his arm brushed up against mine again, and I shuddered. Suddenly, his face was really close to mine, and I moved away. "You little perv. You're trying to kiss me, and I only just met you two seconds ago," Silas laughed again and shook his head.

"I'd argue that it's been way longer than two seconds, but that's your opinion anyway," he said.

"Where's that thing I asked for?" I asked. Silas reached into his pocket, and his arm grazed mine for the third time, but this time I didn't shudder. "Why are you so cold?"

"Uh... I have low iron or something," he said. I'm sure that's a lie, but I dismissed it as I was more concerned about legitimizing his story. I took his timetable and opened it up. I read his full name, and I began to feel my heart pounding in my chest, almost as if it was struggling to jump out. I got up from the bench and put the paper down on the piano.

"Who the hell are you?" I asked angrily. Silas looked at me calmly, like he knew what was going on.

"I'm Silas, the guy you met this morning on the bus," he said calmly. At first, I thought it was just a coincidence that his name was the same as a character in my book, but now I was sure I was being pranked or some weird voodoo shit was happening. Or maybe I was in a dream. Yes, I must've been, because the full name of the Silas in my book was Silas Percy Pushman, and it was all there on his timetable. The first name, fine. I don't doubt that I will never come across a Silas in my life. The last name, Pushman, could be a coincidence, but still really freaky. But all three names? Something weird is happening. I got up from the bench and ran to my locker. I halted in front of it and turned to see him following close behind me. How fast is this guy?

"No! No! No! Stay away!" I screamed as I scrambled to open my locker to retrieve my pepper spray. My plan was dramatic, but I'd rather knock him out and be safe than not knock him out and be dead or assaulted in a couple of seconds. I unlocked my locker and swung the door open, only for it to be swung shut just before I could reach in. I looked at Silas, who was now hovering over me and had his hand on my locker door. I dropped my lock and shook in fear. I tried not to show it, but my hands were trembling uncontrollably.

"How'd you do that?" I asked sternly.

"What do you mean?" He asked.

"You closed my locker without even touching it," I said.

"Don't be silly, Heidi. You're imagining things," he said.

"What did you just call me?" I asked.

"Hei... da... Adelaide... Ade, lady... Ma'lady obviously," he stuttered. The bell rang for the third period and I slowly backed away as the hallway flooded with students.

"Just stay away from me, okay? Please," I said, controlling the shakiness in my voice. I turned around and walked back to the music room to get my stuff. Heidi, he had called me Heidi. Another character in my book, which I wrote based on a better version of myself, using a variation of my own name. She was a version of myself that was strong, badass and a great warrior. One day I dreamt of people who could transform into the different elements, and from there, I created a whole imaginary world of Begavads. That's what I called them. It felt as if my life had finally started once I created that story, and the summer I took to write it was the most alive I had ever felt. The world I made, and the characters I birthed, felt more natural than anything else, but that was just the power of stories. Writers like me know how to stimulate the imagination to create an environment that readers can fall in love with and throw themselves into. My story didn't just feel like a story I wrote. It felt like a story I lived. That is why I wrote the whole novella in a month. It was a short story type and it was currently going through the editing process and on its way to being published. No one has read that book except for me, my mother and my editor. The only living copies are on my computer and a hard copy with my editor. Silas was not my editor, so he must've hacked into my computer and played a sick prank. But for what? Who would do this? Doesn't seem like anyone would gain anything from it unless he's a sadist who just enjoys seeing me rattled.

I tried my best to forget about the whole Silas situation. I have a spare during the fourth period which I often spend in the library. I hadn't seen Silas all day, then I looked up and there he was. I blinked, and all of the sudden, he was beside me and sitting down. I shook my head vigorously. I was in the library alone and the librarian had just stepped out. This would be the perfect time for him to kill me.

"I told you to leave me alone!" I whispered in a stern tone.

"I know, I know, but please, just hear me out. I want to tell you the truth," he said. I knew it. This was all a prank. He hacked my computer. He looks like a hacker even. Well, actually, at first when I saw him, I noticed how toned he was. I thought he might be an athlete, but it makes more sense now that he's a sadistic hacker who likes to prey on paranoid, vulnerable teenage girls. I gave him a nasty look and stayed quiet to allow him to speak. I pulled out my phone and started recording, so I'd have this on record to press charges or get a restraining order or something.

"Heidi, please, I'm not going to hurt you," he said. I continued holding the camera up to his face and glared at him angrily. He then sighed sadly, looked down at the floor and then back at me. "I can't do this anymore. I have to tell you the truth. It's only been a month, but it's so hard not having you around. I know you don't remember, but I'm not just some guy you met on the bus this morning. I've known you for years," I put my phone down in confusion. This guy must be delusional. I think I would remember someone like him.

"You're crazy," I said.

"I know nothing I say will convince you, but you have to trust me. Just ask your mother about the Begavads and the fortress. Ask her about me and CJ. Maybe then you'll remember," he said. And there he went again, naming another character from my book. CJ, the best friend of Adelheid. What is happening?

"CJ?" I asked.

"Yes, yes. CJ, your best friend. Do you remember?" He asked hopefully.

"I'm sorry. I mean... CJ is just another character from my book. I'm writing, or I wrote a book. Listen... I don't even care if you're some sadistic hacker who read my book and is consumed by some kind of Begavad fantasy. I mean, I get it, but this can get really bad if left unchecked. You need help, my dude," I replied. I was no longer scared of Silas if that was even his name. I'm convinced he's a hacker or a superfan. He obviously needs help, and I hope he gets some. I got up and left the library, leaving him behind. I looked back as I walked through the doors and saw him slouched over in his seat. Poor guy, he's cute, but he's crazy.

The bell rang for the end of the school day, and I had finally gotten over the Silas thing completely. I grabbed my bag from my locker and closed it, pulling on the lock twice to assure it was locked properly. Then I left the school, and as I walked down the street to the bus stop, I pulled out my phone to text my mom, getting her ready for the story I was about to tell her about my day at school. I crossed the street. The walk signal was on, but a reckless idiot driver decided that the light wasn't red. He was driving very fast, and I assumed he would stop but he didn't. I was already in the middle of the road. My brain told me to run but my legs stopped moving, and I was crippled. I braced myself, throwing my hands in front of my face as if this would stop me from being run over. I heard the engine of the car revving and felt the exhaust on my open ankles, then I uncovered my face and realized that the car had stopped. I looked to my left at the bus stop, but there was no one there. I looked at the driver in the car, who seemed to be just as shocked as I. He then looked to his left and I followed his gaze to find Silas, holding out his hands, almost as if he had stopped the car himself.

"Move!" He shouted from across the street. I was still in shock, and my heart was beating fast. I finished crossing the street, and I tumbled down on the sidewalk. The car sped away, and Silas was suddenly beside me again. I got up to face him and clutched the pepper spray I concealed in my pocket.

"Give me one good reason why I shouldn't call the cops on you right now?" I asked between deep breaths.

"Well, I just saved your life," he replied, gesturing to where the car had been.

"You've been following me all day," I said. "What are you?"

"You know what I am," he said. I felt like I was in a dream. It wouldn't be too far-fetched to suggest that I, and the idiotic driver who nearly ran me over, just witnessed something completely supernatural. He was freezing cold, fast and could stop vehicles. I would say that he was a vampire, but those aren't real. I couldn't rule anything out at this point. My friends and that driver had seen him, which means he wasn't in my imagination. I figured that all those sleepless nights writing my book were making things hard to understand, so I politely invited Silas to the coffee shop down the street. This was a stupid decision, inviting someone I barely know who had been following me all day for coffee, but he had also saved my life. So though he had been creeping me out all day, I felt the need to thank him. When we got to the shop I asked him what he wanted. He said that he wasn't thirsty so I got myself a large coffee, and we sat ourselves down at a small round table. I looked at Silas smiling at me, then I sucked back half of my coffee. The thing is, he had suddenly appeared to me this morning and was giving me stalker vibes all day. His name was an exact replica of a character in my book, and that wasn't a coincidence. Coincidence was a phenomenon I barely believed in. I trusted more in fate and faith, knowing that everything is planned by a higher power. Even though I should have been disturbed and put off by his presence, I felt an overwhelming closeness to him each time we spoke. It was like no creepy thing he did that day couldn't be solved by a flash of his smile, the sound of his voice or the whip of those brown curly locks. Oh my gosh, he's a witch. I wanted to run away and stare at the same time, but I needed answers before I did either of those first.

"We have about half an hour until this coffee runs its course," I said.

"What does that mean?" He asked.

"Let's just say I'm a little caffeine-intolerant, but I need this to clear my head."

"You know this is our first date. I've always wanted to take you out on a date," he said.

"Right, ever since you met me this morning on the bus, you've just been dying to ask me out," I said sarcastically. Silas laughed and brushed his hands through his curls, proving, again, my theory that every creepy thing he did was cancelled out by his charming personality. I had to stay focused on my mission though and try to ignore his witchcraft. Which, I will admit, I wasn't too clear about with myself. What were my motives for bringing Silas here? Firstly, I had to be absolutely sure I didn't imagine him, and then it would have been nice to get further information about him. With the present data and the made-up reality I created for my book, Silas would be categorized as a water Elemente. A special breed that could also become and manipulate ice because he was always unnaturally cold. His special abilities would include speed and telekinesis, which would explain how he kept on catching up with me and how he stopped a car while its wheels were still moving. It all made sense, except for the fact that it didn't make sense at all, because the reality where that could all be true didn't exist. I explained all this to Silas. He nodded as if he understood and chimed in to tell me that I was correct about his abilities and status.

"It is all real. I know you think you made it up, but what you actually did was write about the life you had before all of this, this reality shift, we're calling it. So, here, let me show you."

He then pulled out a rectangular paper, unfolded it, and slid it towards me. It was a picture of some teens. It looked as though Silas was in it, along with a pale girl with fiery red hair, a younger looking girl in green with bushy hair, and a dark skin boy with a nice buzz cut and one of them looked like me.

"This can't be real," I muttered. "Who took this?"

"Lexin did. He used a real old camera. Something from the 1900s... they had cameras in the 1900s right?" He asked.

"You're asking me? Aren't you the immortal one? Weren't you there?" I questioned.

"What? No! How old do you think I am?" He asked with a chuckle.

"Like 104 years old," I joked.

"I'm 18," he said.

"How long have you been 18?" I asked.

"Um... what? I have been alive for eighteen years. I don't understand the question," he said confusingly.

"You've never seen the movie about the hundred-year-old pedophilic vampire that falls in love with a human teenager?" I asked.

"I'm more of a book person," he said.

"It was based on a book." I said, taking a sip of my coffee.

"I'm not into human teen fiction. That's more my sister's thing," he said.

"GG, right? That's her, with the big hazel hair," I said, pointing to the doe-eyed girl in green. He nodded.

"You remember?" He asked. I shook my head.

"These people look like the ones I made up in my head… perhaps I have been drugged," I theorized. Staring at the picture was surreal. It didn't make any sense. He pulled it away and snatched my coffee. He touched it for a few seconds and then gave it back to me. I opened the lid, and it was completely frozen. I shook my head in disbelief, closed the cup, looked back at him and chuckled.

"That's really cool, but I don't suppose you could unfreeze it because I actually really wanted to drink that," I said. He laughed and shook his head.

"Unfreezing things is more your thing. Why don't you try it?" Silas asked, taking my hands. Although his hands were still freezing cold, he placed my hands on the cup. I leaned in, and he followed suit.

"I'm not a Begavad, you know. I'm not like you," I whispered. "I can't just make things heat up like Adelheid. I can't just make a fire."

"Why would you give the main character of your book your name, the strongest, most powerful Begavad, your name, if you didn't think deep down inside that you were that person?"

"Because it's fun to think that I could be, to imagine a world where I am that royal Begavad, but I'm not," I whispered. "I can't be fire. I can't make fire." And as if I had just summoned it, upon saying those words, my cup burst into flames. I screamed and jumped up from the table, slapping myself on the chest where I felt the flame. The whole coffee shop stopped for a second and stared at me. I pointed at my cup and shouted, "Fire!" Silas took the cup and pretended to pat it out, and it went away. Everyone in the coffee shop returned to their business once the threat was evaded, and I sat back down. My heart was pounding again, and I couldn't believe I had just done that. I could still be going crazy, or Silas could be right. I was the Adelheid from my book. I was fire, water, earth and wind. I was a Begavad.

Arlo Hark

I was approving death certificates for my mother, a tedious task and Begavad law that I hated. As Begavad's, we weren't allowed to hurt or kill Humans. But there was no rule against punishing our own people with the penalty of death. So, it was often the most common punishment that we gave. And as my mother's right hand woman, I had to approve and execute kill orders on criminal Begavads sentenced to death. I didn't like completing this task. But ever since Alira kidnapped my child and never returned, I have been burdened with this title. My mother uses my hate for the work to persuade me to become Queen myself, but I would like nothing more than never to take the throne. I was nearly done reading and approving death certificates. I came across a few ridiculous ones towards the end, but I was too exhausted to go through the paperwork to refuse approval, so I just approved them. I'm sure she ordered them that way on purpose. After I finished, I tried to sneak back to my room when my mother stopped me and asked me to visit the Tapestry Sisters.

"Why do I need to go there now?" I whined.

"I left my ring there. I have lost a bit of weight, you see, and it just slid right off without me noticing. Go fetch it for me," she said, shooing me off.

"I don't even understand why you still wear that thing. It's not like you ever loved my father."

"Oh hush! Just do as I say, that is an order!" She yelled, swooshed her veil and stomped away. That's another thing I can add to the list of things that are a burden because of Alira's disappearance. Alira was a porter, a Begavad who could open portals. Every Queen had a porter. If she wasn't already her right hand woman, usually it was the same person. Alira, being my mother's sister and the only other person who could put up with her, was her right-hand woman and porter. When she left, it all fell onto me, but the problem is I am not a porter. I do not possess the ability to teleport or open up portals. So it is not an understatement when I say it is a burden that has been afflicted upon me.

The Tapestry Sisters resided in Antarctica, a cold and mostly isolated land with a population of 1,000 or so Humans and a couple hundred ice Begavad. I didn't mind the cold, but I still didn't want to take the trip. If I were a porter, it would take me less than a second to get there, maybe five minutes to find my mother's useless ring and another second to get back, but I'm not a porter. To get to Antarctica as a Begavad who does not have the ability to teleport or open portals, I would be taking a 16,000 km trip. That's four hours of flying, if I don't stop for breaks, which seems like a fun adventure, but really after about an hour, your wings get heavy, you're hungry or thirsty, and then you have to pee. Not to mention the risk of being attacked by birds or just the weather in general like rain, hail, snow or even lightning. Luckily there was a clear forecast since it was summer, but that may not be the case when I get to Antarctica. Already, I was wasting too much time dreading the flight, so I decided to start the gruelling task.

When I arrived at the sacred room, I was exhausted. It's the place where they held the tapestry. A lengthy piece of cloth that twisted and turned like a maze all throughout the underworkings of Antarctica that showed the future and past events of Earth. I made it more than halfway through with no sight of the ring. I stopped to see a familiar figure. It was not unusual to come across other Begavads at the tapestry as some with the ability to see would often visit the tapestry to confirm their visions. Still, I was shocked to see someone with our family garments here.

"Mother?" I asked, confused. The woman turned around, and I was taken aback. "What are you doing here?"

"I was just viewing the tapestry for myself, my child. Why are you here?" She asked.

"You sent me here. Remember?" I asked.

"Oh, of course I do. Yes, yes. Well, you know I am getting quite old–"

"Save it," I said, cutting her off. "I know you're not my mother. I can tell the difference, Alira."

"That is aunt Alira to you," she said.

"I have no respect for the woman who stole my child. Where is she?!" I asked angrily.

"She is far and safe," Alira said. I tried using my telepathy to search her mind for my daughter's whereabouts, but she had a strong defence mechanism that prevented me from getting through. "Oh dear, don't hurt yourself. You'll never find her that way."

"Please just give her back," I pleaded.

"She barely knows who you are anymore. There is no point," she said.

"Why are you doing this? Are you working for evil spirits?" I asked.

"Heavens no! I am working for the will of God!" She screamed in offense.

"How so?" I asked.

"I took Harolina so that she would not bring forth the prophecy. Look," she said, turning around pointing to a section of tapestry showing the prophecy that has been spoken about for many years, of a woman who would bring the end of the world, both Human and Begavad. "Do you not see? I am only trying to prevent both the Human and Begavad world's end. When I first took Harolina, this disappeared weeks later, but now it has returned," she turned back around to face me. "The prophecy has been lifted off of Harolina and is now burdening Adelheid, but I will fix it," she said.

"By how? Taking another one of my children? I don't think so," I drew a fiery sword and went into full flame. "I wasn't there to protect my child the first time, but this time I will kill you."

21

"Stop! I beg you!" She said, I wasn't usually one to hesitate. If I drew my sword or any other method of attack, it meant I had thoroughly thought through the repercussions of my actions and had come to the decision that death was the only way. Still, I also didn't enjoy killing people, so I was willing to hear her out. I had a feeling she would be able to justify her actions. "Trust me. This is for the best of us all. I will simply change the tapestry, make it so that you and Adelheid reside in the human world, leaving her with no memories of her Begavad life. Then you can have a chance to be with her, and when the prophecy disappears, I will return Harolina to you. That is what you want, is it not? To be away from the throne, the society, to have a normal, peaceful and loving life with your daughters?" I returned to my flesh form and reduced my sword.

"Fine, but how will you even manage this?" I asked.

"Oh, do not worry about that," she said, so I left her behind. I felt she was truthful in her efforts to evade the horrible fate of the earth, and a few meters passed her, I found the ring, so I saw no further reason to stay. The way I see it, Adelheid and Harolina are a threat to both the Human and Begavad society. Letting them live a human life would not harm either of us. Everything would be fine if she erased their memories. We would evade the deadly prophecy. I saw nothing wrong with this plan, and I have no clue how Alira did it, nor do I want to know how. Yet she did because a week later, I woke up in a human bed, living in a human house, within a gated community located in Thornhill, Ontario. I had no memory of whatever reality I was in now, except for a small sticky note with my address and a message that said, 'Have fun with your new life!' signed Ali. Beside it was a passport and my driving license. All human objects that I had never possessed before. Definitely Alira's work. When I explored my luxurious house, I came across Adelheid's room and saw her sleeping. I watched her sleep as a seventeen year-old girl, just as I did when she was a newborn baby. I remembered how much I missed Adelheid after she left for the anti-fortress and how happy I was to see her now. I remembered how she hated her life before and thought about how much better this one would be for her. I didn't want to wake her, but I couldn't wait to spend time with her in this new world.

Alira Hark

After my encounter with Arlo, I had to find a way to alter the world's fate without killing Adelheid, which I will admit was my original plan until Arlo threatened to kill me, so I immediately went to Australia. Not only was it the land that hosted the most Human criminals, but the most Begavad criminals as well. In fact, most of the criminals there were rogue Begavad. There was no Australian division, so they ran free and unprosecuted. If they were not directly affecting any of the other divisions, none of them saw any reason to get involved. I met up with a half-Martian, half-Human by the 12 Apostles beach and made a request.

"Can you or can you not do this for me?" I asked in a frustrated tone.

"I'm not saying that I can't do it, aight? I'm just sayin' that it's very challenging, and there may be technicalities."

"Like what?"

"Like I can't truly do what you're asking. I can't wipe everyone's memories of the past. That would take me resewing the whole tapestry," she said.

"You were a sewer on Mars. Can you not still execute this action?" I asked.

"Not without getting caught. It would take me years to resew a tapestry that long that would not go unnoticed. So how haven't you been caught anyway?" she asked.

"I suppose Klara was too proud to report me as an enemy of the Begavad society. It would tarnish the Hark name, so I understand why she did not," I explained. "That woman, she would do anything to sustain the Hark name, though she is truly the one who spoils it up until now. I am the only Hark actively fighting to do what is right. Even Arlo, kind and compassionate, is completely misguided by her desires. Oh, how I hate that I share a face with such a wretch! It does not matter. After you do this for me, all will be right."

"Assuming I do it correctly. Remember, I haven't sewn in a millennium, and it took me almost twice that to get back my abilities in full. I'm rusty. I cannot swear that I won't make mistakes."

"I do not care. All that truly matters is that Adelheid has no memory of her fate. That way, it will never come true, even if the others try to convince her otherwise," I said. I put out my hand. She looked down and then shook it.

"Shall I let you know when it is done?" she asked.

"I will be somewhere where you cannot reach me, but I will be able to feel when the change is made. Just do your part," I said, and then I teleported back to Harolina.

Silas Pushman

When I awoke from my sleep, I noticed that Adelheid was not in her bed. I assumed that she had just gotten up before me, so I hopped out of bed and called her name. No answer. I went back to my room and got ready for the day. Then I went to the cafeteria for breakfast, and to my surprise, everyone was there except for Adelheid. I sat down at the table and asked the group where she was. "Maybe she's at the pool," CJ suggested. "Did you check the practice room?"

"Ya, on the way here. She never skips breakfast," I said. I thought it was weird that she woke up so early, but it didn't seem too unusual. Heidi was a model student and waking up early to get a head start on training was a very Alpha thing to do. I applaud her for getting used to this schedule before I did. It's been three years at the anit-fortress and I still haven't adjusted to waking up at 6 am and being yelled at and berated by Lexin. For the first two years here, we focused more on learning about our history like we did at the fortress, and then we learned about Mars and their world. Now we mostly train for hours and hours. Today was different, though. Today felt off. Maybe it was just because I didn't wake up with Heidi next to me.

When we finished breakfast, we went to the practice room, where we were greeted by Lexin's anxiously tapping foot.

"We have an issue. One of you is missing," he said, and he was right. Heidi was late, but she was never late. "Silas, I am assigning you on a rescue mission."

"Rescue mission? For who? Heidi?" I asked. Lexin nodded.

"What? But she was literally just here yesterday," CJ said.

"Yes, and now she has vanished," Lexin said.

"Okay, but did you check the pool?" Mike asked.

"Yes, and the classroom, and the library and the den, twice. She is not here, but I do know where she might be," Lexin said. He projected a map of Ontario.

"Why is she in the land of the Humans?" I asked.

"I do not have all the details because the Tapestry Sisters locked down the sacred room. What I do know is the tapestry has been tampered with, and it directly resulted in the reality of Adelheid. Now, she is there, and I am sure she has no recollection of what has happened, or she would likely be here," Lexin explained. "I cannot give you an exact location as Klara is making it very difficult for me. She gave me a general idea and told me it was my responsibility to find her. I'm sure she knows where she is, but she is just being difficult. Anyways, Silas, you will go and retrieve her."

"We should all go," CJ said.

"No, this is a one person job," Lexin said.

"What if whoever took Heidi is dangerous?" CJ asked.

"No one took Adelheid. She was relocated when reality shifted, but whoever did this was obviously too stupid or completely unskilled with the ways of the tapestry and forgot to wipe our memories too. So only Adelheid was affected. Also, Adelheid is not alone. She is with her mother."

"Does she have memories of the reality shift?" I asked.

"Unclear, she's disconnected from the telepathic network, but if she does not, she should be easy to take down," Lexin said.

"I'm not going to fight my girlfriend's mother," I said.

"Relax, she likely will not attack you unless she feels threatened, but that doesn't matter. Ontario is a big place. You'll have to find them first, and then we will deal with that," Lexin said.

"Why can't I just zoom in and zoom out?" I asked.

"I cannot risk you showing yourself to the Humans, you will have to disguise yourself as one," Lexin said. He gave me a human device and some clothes and then confiscated my suit. "I cannot have you tempted to form while you are amongst the Humans."

Lexin would not allow me to use my super-speed to run to Ontario, so I had to use a car that he hadn't driven since the 1900s. I mentioned that if his goal were to make sure I went unnoticed, this car would surely blow it. I told him that it was too old and probably didn't even work, but he told me to shut up and take it anyway. It did work, but it was still old and drew a lot of attention. The drive from Arizona to Ontario was a whole day without stops. Of course, I took it like a champ and held my pee until I arrived at the border. It took me two weeks to track down Heidi and her mother. They were located in Thornhill, in a gated community, with humans. I found them by visiting a similar gated community in Oakville. This particular one was home to many Begavad families who worked in human affairs. I asked around until I finally found a telepath who could give me the exact location of Adelheid and her mother. When I finally made it to Heidi's new home, I knocked on the door. Lexin had told me to survey the area first, but I was sure this way would be faster. I just wanted to see if either of them remembered me. When the door opened, I was greeted by Arlo, Heidi's mother.

"You need to leave here now," she said.

"So you know who I am?" I asked her.

"Yes, Silas, I know who you are," she said, as she closed the door behind her. "Listen. Heidi is going to be happier here, okay?"

"Happier without me?" I asked.

"Silas, I do truly like you, so don't make me hurt you," she said. I stepped back. I wanted to form and draw a sword, but if I did, my clothes would be soaked since Lexin confiscated my suit and made me change into Human clothes. Not to mention that Arlo could easily overpower me, so I stood down.

"It's been weeks, Arlo. Lexin is getting agitated. He says a threat is coming. We need her, she's a part of our team."

"I know, but she's doing so well here. She's writing, making friends, living a regular teenage life, going to school next week too. She's happy, truly happy. Lexin could just let one of the Beta teams deal with this one."

"Are you the one who tampered with the tapestry?" I asked.

"No, but I didn't stop it," she said. "Now leave, please," I nodded and obeyed her orders. I drove down the street and stopped in a grocery store parking lot. I then pulled out my messenger and proceeded to call Lexin.

"Why are you not using the Human device I provided you with?" Lexin asked.

"It died, like three hours ago," I said.

"How? Were you playing games on it?" he asked.

"No! I don't play games. I just had it sitting on the seat the whole time," I said.

"What! In the sun?" he asked. I nodded. "Those Human devices are not susceptible to heat."

"Well, how am I supposed to know that?" I asked.

"You should have learned this in… Ugh, never mind. Do you have something to report?" he asked.

"Yes, I do. So I had an encounter with Arlo, and she told me to leave, very politely, might I add," I reported. Lexin then proceeded to yell at me, reminding me that I disobeyed his orders and that was not what he had told me to do. In the end, he finally calmed down and said to wait for Heidi to be alone. He sent me the bus route and address of Heidi's human school and told me to retrieve her from there delicately.

"Do not make a scene! It is crucial that you mind my words, boy! Anything you do out there will affect the Human world, and the Begavad society already has a lot of cleaning up to do," he warned. I reminded Lexin that I was not a boy as I was eighteen years old and promised to follow his instructions this time. Then I checked into a Begavad-owned Human hotel.

"Please keep in mind that this is a Human hotel. I welcome you here free of charge, but if you show yourself to the humans, I will have to kick you out. So, please be mindful of my rules," the fellow Begavad said as he let me into a room in the basement.

"Thank you sir. You have my word, sir," I said. I waited for a week, surveilling Heidi and her mother. When I saw her pause or stop or look around, I would get a slight chill down my back every time, almost as if she knew I was watching her.

CHAPTER TWO

Arlo Hark hadn't seen her husband Jake in a year. The reason being Begavad custom to keep mothers-to-be and sickly patients segregated from the rest of society. Somehow along the way the Begavad society felt the need to completely detach themselves from the Human race. They had already segregated and hidden, but they also wanted to destroy everything that made them human. It never became an official law, as it is almost impossible to outlaw emotions, but those who showed fear, sadness, frailty, or love were heavily looked down upon and sometimes even shunned. Especially if their emotions got in the way of a mission. In that case, it could be grounds for execution. So the Begavad society became one that cringed at the sight of affection. Mothers didn't hug their children, and no one would ever dare shed a tear when someone died. Of course this all changed with Arlo's generation and it only got worse with Adelheid's. Still, to this day, I haven't seen her cry. And so, all mothers-to-be are confined in the hospitality ward at the start of their second trimester, up until a week after birth. Many healers worked in the hospitality ward and were sworn to secrecy on who and what occurred, though it was quite obvious if you had ever been there yourself.

Arlo and Jake were allowed a few moments alone with their children before they were presented to the people. Arlo and

Jake smiled at their twins, Adelheid and Harolina. Suddenly the doors opened noisily and Alira, Klara's sister, walked towards the babies to admire them.

"The twins are beautiful. Their power is so strong. I can sense it. Yes, it will be a great battle to decide who shall be Queen," Alira exclaimed.

"Well, we're hardly thinking about that. The twins haven't even learned to open their eyes yet," Arlo said.

"I know, I know. I just see, I see… Oh…" Alira's face went pale with this remark and she continued to marvel at the twins.

"What? What's wrong? Are you seeing something bad?" Arlo asked. Alira shook her head and smiled. She reluctantly pushed out a fake little laugh and then nodded her head.

"No, no, no. It's simply just the burdens of my old age. Nothing is wrong. I'm only here to inform you that it is time for you to get dressed. The ceremony will be starting very soon." Alira said. However, this was partially a lie. It was true that the ceremony was to begin soon, but Alira had lied when she told Arlo that her shocked expression was due to her old age. Alira was old, but she was not nearly old enough to start feeling it in such a way that she was expressing. The truth was that Alira had seen something horrible when she gazed upon the children. Particularly when she set eyes on Harolina, the firstborn, by a matter of five minutes. What Alira had seen as she gazed upon Harolina lined up with the image she had seen sewn into the tapestry the night she visited the Tapestry Sisters. The Tapestry Sisters were triplets, burdened with the abilities to see, sew and protect the tapestry that held the outline of the world's fate, including its past, present and future. Alira, being a seer herself, often visited the tapestry to understand her visions.

When you are a seer, like Alira, you get bits and pieces of the possibilities that lie in the future. But to confirm what could be, you must consult the tapestry and this is what Alira had done a night before the ceremony. She had seen decades into the future. She had seen the gruesome fate of the human race, and felt sorry for them. As she realized what horrid contributions Harolina would make to their ruin, she quickly concocted a plan to change their fate.

"Okay, we'll go. But Amona, do tend to the children." With that Arlo and Jake left the room. Alira continued to stare at the babies as Amona came towards her. Then, without a glance behind her, Alira sprung her hand up.

"Halt there, Amona. Take a break. I'll tend to the children. Leave this place," Alira said. Amona left the room suspiciously. Amona was a wise nurse, meaning she knew something unsettling was about to happen without telepathic or seeing abilities. She was one of those Pentaelkays that had the potential to develop new abilities throughout her life. With this wisdom and suspicion, she quickly ran to the Queen's chambers, where Klara patiently waited for her children to be ready for the ceremony.

"You are frightened. You have something important to tell me that cannot wait until the end of the ceremony. I will listen. Speak!" Klara stated as she read her mind. It would have been faster for Klara to read Amona's mind further, but she respected privacy and only used her telepathic powers for urgent matters, like deciding whether killing Amona for bursting into her room on such an important day was just or not. Such an act was usually punishable by extreme consequences in other circumstances.

"I truly do not wish to burden you with even more stress than you knowingly have on such a sacred day, but I came to make you aware of the unsettling feeling I had as I left the hospitality room that your granddaughters occupy. This feeling was rooted in the presence of your sister."

"My sister? What was Alira doing there?"

"She came to inform Arlo and Jake of the timely ceremony and told them to get ready. Then told me to leave. That is when I knew something was wrong."

"I feel it too. Oh, I must hurry!" With that, Klara formed into a gust of wind and swiftly moved as fast as one into Arlo's room just as Klara picked up one of the babies. She then took back her bodily form to face her sister.

"What are you doing?" Klara snapped. Alira carefully turned around to mind the newborn in her arms and smiled gracefully at Klara.

"I will protect you, and thus, I will protect the fate of this Earth that these fools tarnish," she whispered to the baby. "I'm taking her away, somewhere where you cannot find her."

"And why would you do that?"

"Oh, you know," she said as she slowly rocked the baby. "You must have seen the tapestry. The latest developments in Earth's fate, it is a horrid one!"

"It has always been."

"No, it has not! It was always meant to be glorious, that is what we swore to protect. They are all meant to go to heaven so they will be with their Father."

"And they still will."

"Not if we are here."

"Surely it will be delayed, but just as surely it will play out. We cannot change the inevitable future."

"But somehow, you have found a way."

"Okay, I am done talking. Put the baby back where you found her, or your fate will come much sooner than you saw." Klara formed a fiery bow and arrow from her hands and became ready to shoot.

"I am doing God's will."

"No! You are doing the will of evil!"

"How dare you?!" Klara took a shot, but Alira's eyes saw too quickly, and she vanished just as the arrow grazed one of the baby's eyes. At that moment, Klara felt a forbidden feeling of sadness, as she prided herself to be the most skilled Begavad on Earth, yet she had missed her shot. She had no similar emotions for the child that had just been stolen from Arlo and Jake. She paid no attention to the worried parents who had just entered the room.

"Well, at least we still have one," Klara said as she walked towards the baby and picked her up.

"What? Well, where is the other?" Arlo asked, confused.

"She was taken... by Alira," Klara stated without a trace of emotion. Arlo and Jake looked at each other in shock.

"Well... What will we tell the people?" Arlo asked, fighting back the tears. Jake took her hand for comfort. Klara turned around and frowned.

"Do not cry for her! She is gone, and she never existed," Klara screeched angrily.

"But I made her. If someone had taken me at such a young age, would you not cry for me?" Arlo asked.

"Do you think God cries every time a creature of his dies or is lost to Him?" Klara asked with a harsh glare.

"I would hope so," Arlo said confidently, now feeling angrier towards her mother's carelessness than sad for the newborn she had just lost.

"Well, what a Queen you will be," Klara said as she made her way to the door. She then stopped and turned to the couple and Amona, who had followed them back to the baby's room. "We will tell the people that there will be a new heir to the throne. And you, Arlo, you gave birth to this child. Singular. My daughter, Arlo, heir to the throne when I pass on my reign. You have had one child, a proud Begavad named…" Klara then waited for her to state the name.

"Adelheid, that one was named Adelheid," she said.

"That one? There was only ever one," Klara said. Arlo sucked on her lips as she fought back the tears again. "Oh, stop it! The ceremony will start now." And so it did. They had the ceremony, the people cheered and blessed the child. Then it ended, and instead of crying in each other's arms, Arlo and Jake simply stared at the child and wondered what had happened to the other one. They were too afraid to ask the Queen. This fear, plus the passing of Jake, haunted Arlo for the rest of her life. It took her many years to get over it. Arlo was Queen for a number of two weeks until Klara deemed her unfit due to her depressive nature. So Klara remained Queen, and Arlo yearned for her lost child as she tried her best to love and care for the only one she had left.

___

Arlo Hark

That night Adelheid and I sat in the living room for hours as I told her the story of her heartless grandmother and how she ruined the fate of the world. I told her about her father, who passed on his immortality to her and how much he loved her. I told her about her grandmother's strict rules on emotions, and the Begavads do's and don'ts. I did not tell her about Harolina or her aunt. I only said that Alira was lost to us and had messed with the tapestry in an effort to fix what my mother had done and, in turn, had messed up her fate and put her in a new reality. Of course most of this was a lie and didn't make much sense, but she was shocked and dazed by the information and trauma of her near-death experience, that she didn't ask many questions.

"Wow... that's a lot," she said. "I guess I had to know some of what you were telling me because I wrote a whole book about it."

"I know. I was so proud of you when you told me you wrote a book. I thought you were on your way to having a normal human life, but when I read it, I noticed that you were just writing about your life," I said. "I thought soon you would be back to being miserable again and being out of place."

"Well, I was writing about my life, and I didn't even know it."

"Do you recall anything?" I asked.

"No, but I've always felt like something was missing. On my way home today, I noticed that I don't remember anything from my early childhood. Last week I went to May's sweet sixteen, and I was trying to remember mine, but I couldn't really recall any details. I assumed I had one, but I wasn't sure," she said and then shrugged. "I don't know. It's just one of those memorable moments that I had seemed to forget, but it seemed weird since it would've only been a year."

"That's because this reality was literally created a month ago. Your grandmother has been trying to fix it, but she is not getting anywhere. You don't remember your sweet sixteen because Begavads don't celebrate birthdays. You never had one. I was forbidden to even bake you a cake." Heidi looked down for a second and shook her head. I could see the wheels turning as she tried to process the information and absurdity of it all.

"Why do you think Aunt Alira did this?" she asked. I opened my mouth to speak and then paused for a second. I knew why Alira did it. I didn't disagree with her at all. Yet, I couldn't tell Heidi that because then I would have to tell her about her sister. I did not want her wanting or chasing after something that was lost to us or resenting me for not having the guts to find her myself.

"I don't know. Your aunt left when you were born. Who knows why she came back to disturb your life. All I know is that I am sorry. Not because she did this, but because you have to go back to a life I know you never wanted," I said.

"Well, can't I just not go back? I mean, I don't even remember. I would be useless," she said.

"No, you must. I know it's not fair, but you were born into this life. We all were. At least you won't be around my cursed mother."

"What do you mean?" she asked.

"Well, your grandmother is punishing you and your team for things my team and I did in our youth. So you will be living and training at Ununseptium Labs with Lexin, just as my team and I did when my mother banished us," I said as I shook my head in anger. I pulled Heidi close and gave her a hug of comfort. I made sure to hug her at least twice a day ever since this new reality came to be, and before this, I always told her I loved her. My mother never did these things. She was rarely around because she was constantly fulfilling her duties as Queen, and when my mother was around, she would only talk about how I would have to be when I became Queen. She was obsessed with her power. She thinks she's doing everything right, her and the whole Begavad council, but her rules are stupid and misguided. I believe that the Begavads were never like this in the beginning. We weren't meant to be cold, heartless, killing machines. My beliefs are why I rejected the throne and the only reason why my mother is still Queen. She thinks that after Jake passed and Harolina was taken, I became depressed, but I was always depressed. She didn't take the throne from me because of that. I let her take it because I hoped it would mean that Adelheid would be free from it. Though she still believes we are flawed. Not allowing Adelheid to be Queen would be straying too far from the Begavad way. My hope for Adelheid is that she will have the courage to do what I couldn't, step up as Queen and return the Begavad society to what it used to be. Although, I fear that her fate won't allow it. Adelheid pulled away from me and then smiled.

"I think I'm ready," she said. Although she had no idea what lay ahead, her book, though entertaining, didn't even skim the surface of how mentally and physically draining it was to train to be a Begavad.

"Tomorrow. Until then, sleep and enjoy your last twelve hours of normal," I said. She smiled again and then went upstairs. I sat on the couch for a couple more hours staring at the wall, just like I did when Alira took Harolina away from me.

CHAPTER THREE

Ununseptium Labs was an underground facility that could only be accessed through an invisible entrance in a rock that led to an elevator and took you way underground. It had a pool, weight room, cafeteria and five bedrooms, not including Lexin and his assistant Lilian's room. It also had a lab, Lexin's lab. No one was allowed in there, not even Lilian. Especially not her. Lilian was Lexin's assistant, but he was also like a father figure to her. She was a Martian who had her powers taken away as she was banished to Earth. At the time of her banishment, Ununseptium Labs served as a refuge for Martian immigrants thrown off the planet. Lilian's circumstance was different because she had just committed mass murder on her planet in an attempt to avenge her father, whom terrorists had killed, but this is not her story. It is barely relevant to this case, so I won't get into it. The point is Lilian and Lexin were close. But even she wasn't allowed into his lab because it held dark secrets that would probably make Lilian look down on him. Lexin was an Alpha Begavad and a direct descendant of Zazo Lambois, one of the first five Begavads. Lexin was ancient. He was only the third generation from his family line, making him about 125 years old, but he only looked like he was in his 40s. This was because of the things he did in his lab—illegal Begavad experimentation. Klara, the Queen, always knew he was sketchy. So when he came to the fortress years ago proposing a Martian immigration asylum, she immediately banished him. She did things like this often. Having the resources that any Alpha Begavad has, he decided to create the asylum himself in the middle of the desert. It then became Ununseptium Labs after the Begaved council restricted earth as a dumping ground for Mars. Even though Klara found Lexin shady, she still gave him the responsibility to train and teach her daughter, Arlo, and her team, the Begavad way. Though I'm sure she truly just threw them to him because she didn't want them around in the fortress. Lexin did a good job preparing Arlo and her team for any possible threats. Still, there were never any major problems that needed solving in their time. Lexin became quite bored and thus began experimenting on himself even more. It is natural for every Begavad to have one or more elements and a special ability or two. Lexin, however, had more than five special abilities, which made him entitled and very sought after by higher beings. His abilities included telekinesis, telepathy, speed, teleportation, increased strength, flight and many more. He was also an Alpha Begavad, so he possessed all four elements of earth, fire, water and air. He was almost unstoppable. But now that Adelheid was back, his time as the most powerful Alpha Begavad was coming to an end once again. If he were here, I feel the events that are about to unfold would not be a problem, but he's not because he's dead. Really, truly dead.

Adelheid Hark

When I woke up the following day, my mother was standing by my bedroom door. Usually, I would find this creepy, but under the circumstances, I understood. Especially after she told me that I wasn't going to see her for a long while. I attempted to pack a bag before leaving, but Silas advised me not to.

"You'll have everything you need back at the Labs," he said after my mother had said her goodbyes. She didn't want to see me go, so she left before I did.

"I don't suppose we'll be flying there?" I asked.

"Come on, you know I can't fly yet," Silas said lightly. "Don't rub it in."

"Right, sorry. I would know that because that's totally normal for people not to be able to fly," I said as we walked down the stairs. I stopped at the door just as Silas exited the house. "It feels so weird to leave this big house with nothing on my back."

"It'll take some getting used to, but you'll get it all back eventually," he said. I got into his vintage car, and we drove for hours. I tried to sleep, but I mostly just thought about the 'what if's.' What if I didn't get it all back? What if I could never be the same person I was? The same person I wrote about in that book. Why am I talking like any of this is even possible?

When we finally made it to Ununseptium Labs, I met the team. I recognized all the faces from the photo. The pale girl with the red hair, CJ. Silas' little sister with the bushy hazel hair, and Mike, the dark skin boy. I got a tour of the Labs, though I felt that I didn't need it, as everything felt very familiar to me.

"I will let you get settled in. Your teammates will help you out," Lexin said as he and Lilian walked away. CJ and Silas stood beside me and stared at me with anxious smiles. The vibes were awkward and mildly uncomfortable. Partly from me not fully knowing how to be around people I thought I created and them not knowing how to act around an amnesia patient.

"So you don't remember anything, huh?" CJ asked. I shook my head. "That really sucks. I wish you knew how much I missed you."

"Here, let's show you your room," Silas said, grabbing my hand. I glanced at him weirdly. "Um, it's activated with a unique handprint. Usually, you would use your element, but Lexin set it, so it just uses your fingerprints for now." I put my hand up to the pad next to my door, and it clicked. I turned the handle and was delighted to see that my room had a great deal of space.

"This room seems way bigger than the other ones," I said.

"Ya, the captain's quarters are always bigger than the other rooms. Even at the fortress," Silas said. I stepped into my room and pulled out my phone. I had brought it out of habit.

"Oh ya, you're not gonna need that," CJ says.

"Y'all don't have phones?" I asked. This rule certainly wasn't in my book. I guess I missed some things.

"There's no need for them unless you're one of those Begavads that are always in human affairs. There is no need for any type of device, except for the basic communicator Lexin will give you. Lexin doesn't really mind, but he doesn't see the point in them honestly. They are strictly prohibited at the fortress," CJ said.

"Plus, you won't have time to use it because you will be training 24/7. Every day of your long, long, long, endless immortal

Begavad life for threats that may never appear," Silas said, almost sarcastically.

"Well, that just sounds great. I can't wait to be a Begavad," I said air quoting the word Begavad. "I'm already homesick." I flopped down on my back onto my bed, and CJ sighed, then turned to Silas.

"Maybe try to jog her memory. Remind her of her life. I'm going to go… stare at the wall for the fifth time today and contemplate running away again," CJ said jokingly to Silas. With that, CJ left my room closing the door, and Silas sat on the edge of my bed.

"Is she okay?" I asked.

"Ya, she's fine. That's just CJ. I mean, she's a little depressed, but who wouldn't be when trapped in the desert," he said. I can't help but think that that'll be me in a few days. Or maybe it was me, is me? I sat up and shuffled beside him. Our hands touched, and I looked up at him embarrassingly.

"Sorry," I said, shuffling away.

"No it's okay," he said quickly. I moved back over a bit. "You know we were really close before."

"In my book, Adelheid was Silas' love interest… I was your love interest. Or you were mine, I should say. I know how I wish Silas or you felt about me, I mean, I know how I wrote it, but I guess I was right. I mean, how close were we?" I asked. Silas smiled and pushed back a lock of hair from his face.

"I've always had a crush on you, even before we came here and talked about running away to the human world to go on a real date one day," he said shyly.

"So we were dating?" I asked.

"Or at least trying too. Dating isn't really a thing with Begavads. When Begavads are born especially, Begavads like you, like royalty, you know, heir to the throne and all that, a suiter is chosen, usually at birth," he said. I nodded. "For simple Begavad commoners like me, I get the choice of two to three different girls. But for royalty, you're looking at an arranged marriage."

"I get it. Gotta keep the bloodline strong and pure," I said.

"Eh, not really. I think it's just a snobby royalty thing. No offense," he said.

"No offense taken. I don't even know who I am, and considering my mother had described my grandmother as a heartless evil being, I'm not sure I even want the throne," I said. "So, are you one of my suitors?"

"Don't know. As far as I know, your mother hasn't decided yet, but I'm sure she would want you to be with who you want. She's untraditional like that."

"She does seem like quite the rebel," I said. "So what if I want you?"

"You do, or you did, but you don't even remember your feelings for me," he said.

"I know, but I remember what I wrote about your character," I said.

"I doubt your book is an exact representation of who I am. In fact, I know it's not, because I read it. I'm not a character in your book Adelheid, I'm real," he said. That was the problem. He was a real guy, who was interested in me. Who liked me. And because of Alira, I don't get to remember whatever type of relationship I had with him. He seemed perfect. At least that's how I wrote him in my book. But he was right. He wasn't a character in my book, he was a real person and I wanted a real relationship with him, or at least I thought I did. Either way, now I have to start over. I don't know if I'll be able to keep him. I have zero experience with boys, and even though I am technically Adelheid, I don't feel like her.

"So help me remember us. No first date because Begavads don't do that, but have we had our first kiss?" I asked shyly. Silas gave a smug smirk and then laughed a little.

"A first, a third and many more," he said embarrassingly. "But don't make me blush." "Uh, okay, have we ever, ya know," I said, giving him a weird eye gesture that my deluded mind thought he'd understand. He shook his head in confusion. "Ya know like s–"

"Oh…" he said, cutting me off. "No. Abstinence is highly stressed here. Here and in the fortress."

"Interesting," I said, glad that I hadn't forgotten anything meaningful, I sighed. "I feel like I've missed so much." Silas came closer to me and put his hands on mine. He was still bitterly cold, but now I knew why I didn't mind it.

"Don't worry, Lexin has a lab. We're not allowed to go in there, but I know he's working on something to help you. Sooner or later, things will go back to the way they were," Silas said. Despite my absence of memory, I suddenly felt a closeness to Silas. I rested my head on his shoulder. He was comforting to be around. "You really didn't miss that much, to be honest. We only just started training. I haven't even been able to hold my form for more than a few seconds. None of us can."

I had almost forgotten why I was here. Being with Silas made me forget everything, which was nice.

I remembered what my mom had told me about Begavad abilities and that forming was an action that Begavads did with their element. Forming allowed one to become their element, and it was also the only way to heal from any affliction. Silas and I continued to talk all night in my room about what happened in my other life, theories of why my aunt did what she did. He also told me all about his childhood growing up with his little sister GG and Mike after his mom passed. Everything felt so natural with him, and I wasn't totally bothered by the fact that I might have to spend the rest of my life in the desert, training for threats that may never appear.

Lilian Herma

I woke up to the sound of an agonizing scream. It was 2 am, and I wondered if an intruder was disrupting the children. I slid out of bed feeling uneasy and a little scared. I quickly shuffled to Lexin's room, and before I had the chance to knock, I noticed the door was open. So, I stuck my head in and called out to him. The room was pitch black. When I did not hear a response, I opened the door. The screaming had stopped. When I flicked on the light, Lexin was not in his room. Then I heard the scream again. I now realized that it was coming from the lab. It must have been Lexin. I ran up to the lab doors with the intent to help him, but then I stopped to think. Lexin constantly reminds me to think. He says 'think about what you are doing, Lilian. Do not let your emotions control your actions, Lilian.' He always says that. I know Lexin can take care of himself, but as I heard him scream once more, I shook my head at the thought of crawling back to bed and hacked into the keypad to unlock the door. Lexin was lying on the ground clutching his head, and as I closed the door to approach him, he started to scream again. I kneeled to comfort him and evaluated his situation.

"Are you hurt? What is wrong? Why are you screaming?" I questioned. Lexin shook his head, squinted his eyes, and pointed at the syringe on the desk. "What do you want me to do?" He winced in pain and pointed to the inside of his right arm. Rushingly, I got up, snatched the syringe and proceeded to inject the solution into his arm. His face was all scrunched up and it looked like he was about to cry, but then after a few seconds, he became relaxed and got up from the floor.

"What just happened, Lexin? What are you doing here, so late?" I asked.

"It is none of your concern. Leave at once," Lexin dismissively stated as he got up from the ground and started organizing his desk, which had previously been in disarray. I got up angrily and stomped over to him, folding my arms in the process.

"What do you mean it is none of my concern? That is a concern when you are out here screaming in the middle of the night." I said sternly.

"Lilian now is not the time to talk about this. There are bigger problems at hand," he said.

"What problems?" I asked.

"Well, for one, we are about to be attacked," he mumbled.

"By whom? And how do you know such things?" I asked.

"Lilian, now is really not the time. Please, go back to bed," he said. I stared into his eyes. He would not give me the slightest clue as to why he was screaming or why we would be under attack. I rolled my eyes and decided to give up. I would figure out what he was doing tomorrow.

Lexin Lambois

Last night Lilian found me lying on the floor in my lab, screaming and she was concerned. I had not scorned her yet for coming into my lab when she knew it was off-limits. The keypad coded to my specific handprint should signify that no one else is allowed to enter, but she still got in. Lillian ripped off the keypad and hacked it via the wires. I always knew she was smart enough to do something like that, but I thought she would respect my boundaries and rules. After that dramatic scene, I upgraded the lab's security system. I plan on reeducating Lilian on the importance of thinking before doing and being respectful. It is not all her fault. When I got her, she was already mostly fully grown and had the way of her people already instilled in her. I did my best to teach her the ways of the Earthly Begavad, but she can only retain so much. As I approached my lab, my jaw almost dropped to the floor. The door had been completely burned off by some type of acid and was expelling smoke. I can not believe she would go this far to get into my business. Nonetheless, I stepped into the lab and found her reading one of my latest journals next to my desk.

"What the hell do you think you are doing?" I asked angrily.

"Me?! What are you doing Lexin?" Lilian asked, mirroring my anger. She looked up at me and held up the journal to my face. "You might have written this in code Lexin, but as you know I am very smart and I figured it out."

"It is not code, it is an Earthly language called Swedish," I said.

"I do not care! Why are you experimenting on yourself?" she asked.

"No." I protested. Lillian's frown slowly turned into a pout, and her eyes began to water. "Oh, please do not cry. It is so not Begavad, and it physically pains me to see it, and not in a good way."

"Lexin, you know that I care very much about you, and you are like a father to me. I have already lost my biological father, and I barely got to know him. So when I hear you screaming in the middle of the night and then asking me to inject you with some mystery serum, well... well, I am sorry I do not want to see you die as well."

"Fine, just please do not cry. It makes me so uncomfortable," I pleaded. "Last night, I had a weird feeling in my gut. It was a feeling I had been having for a few weeks, and this feeling was telling me that something bad was going to happen. It made me think how useful it would be if I were ten steps ahead of our enemies. So I gave myself the power to see. It came all at once, hence the screaming, but I would have gotten through it eventually on my own. So, there was no reason for you to break into my lab."

"What? You were screaming! You sounded like you were in pain. Where did you even get this seeing power from?" she asked.

"Classified." I said. Lilian huffed and then snatched a conveniently placed lighter from off my desk. She held the lighter up to my journal, and my gut almost dropped out of me.

"Lilian, no, wait!" I said, fearful of my precious thoughts and research. "Ok. I will tell you the truth. The seeing power was extracted from a Martian, alright?"

Lilian put down the lighter and threw the book at my chest. I caught it and held onto it tightly.

"Like the Arspens? You took powers from innocent Martian's for yourself? How many?"

"Well they were hardly innocent."

"How many Martian abilities did you steal, Lexin?!" She said angrily as she raised her voice.

"Seven or ten. I have lost count, if I am being honest," I said. Lilian looked at me in shock and started to back away. "A year after I accepted you into my home, word had gotten to Mars that you were safe and sound on Earth. I guess this angered them, and they started sending Martian authorities to collect and kill you. Well, as you can see, I never let that happen. So instead, I killed them, extracted their power and put them back on Mars."

"So I guess you can teleport now too," she asked rhetorically.

"They were going to kill you, Lilian. And I had started to get used to you being around and thought that it might be detrimental to the immigration asylum I had created if you were gone." I said.

"Fine. Thanks for letting me live, but why did you never give my powers back? If you were just extracting from all these Martians, surely you saved something for me," she said hopefully. I walked over to my bookshelf filled with past journals. I pulled on a faux journal to the left on the second shelf. The bookshelf opened up to reveal an entire wall of vials with abilities I had extracted from Martians who had come to take Lilian. I had not used them all for myself. Mostly because some were duplicates of ones I had already acquired, and taking them would not increase my power. So I saved them, but not for Lilian.

"This is everything I have extracted over the many years I have been watching over and protecting you. This wall represents all the Martians on your planet who sought to kill you. So do not cry for them, Lilian. What you did was wrong and pointless, but you have to move on from that." I said. Lilian nodded.

"Well, could I have my teleporting powers back and maybe some more?" she asked kindly. I shook my head and sighed. "Why not?!"

"Lilian, when you first came here and told me what had happened, I thought it was due to your temperamental teenage tendencies. I assumed you would grow out of it naturally, but you did not. You are way too unstable to possess such abilities. You never think. You use your emotions to dictate your actions, which is never a smart move. For this reason, I cannot with good conscience allow you to have your powers back." I said. I then moved closer towards Lilian. "And if you ever step foot in my lab again, I will not stop the next Martians who come down here to collect you. I will let them take you, and I will not shed a tear." Lilian looked at me angrily and shook her head as she walked away. Without me, she was defenceless. Even without my extra abilities, I was one of the most powerful Begavad there was. I know my threat would keep her out of the lab, not that she knows how to break in discretely, and now I need a new door.

CJ (Claire-Joan) Johnson

Today was going to be a good day. I just knew it. Today was going to be the day I finally formed. I had been practicing all last night. I was so eager to be the first one from my team to do it. I was also happy that Adelheid was back. Everything is less bleak when she's around. I decided to greet Adelheid in her room and walk her to the cafeteria for breakfast. As I walked down the hall, I noticed Silas had left his door wide open, and he was not in his room. Then I got to Adelheid's room and her door was cracked, so I took it as an invitation to come in. As I turned on the lights, I saw Adelheid and Silas passed out on the edge of the bed. How cute.

"Well, I hope I am not disturbing anything," I shouted as they sprung up. Adelheid looked around in confusion, and Silas hopped up and zoomed out. As he passed me, I nearly got knocked off my feet. I hate when he does that.

"We were talking all last night. Must've fallen asleep," she said.

"No problem. None of my business, really. I just wanted to say good morning and walk you down to the cafeteria for breakfast." I said. Adelheid got up and gave me a smile.

"Ya sure, just let me get ready," she said, heading to the bathroom.

"Hey, have you seen your closet yet?" I asked.

"Ah no. Didn't do much exploring last night," she said from the bathroom.

"It's pretty cool and one of the perks of being here and not at the fortress. Lilian hand-makes all our clothes just for us and our elements. You'd get handmade clothes in the fortress too, but there isn't quite as good of a seamstress as Lilian. They're made that way so your clothes don't burn off when you form into fire, or so you're not soaked after you form into water. And they're fashionable." I explained.

"That's cool," she said, stepping out of the bathroom. Adelheid opened up her closet and surveyed the outfits. "Everything's purple, though."

"Ya well, purple is your colour. All my clothes are red. All of Silas' are blue, GG's are green and brown, and Mikes are white and grey." I said. "To match your element."

"I guess I never noticed that. So what colour does Lexin wear? Black?" she asked. I nodded. "And I guess Lilian only wears white then?"

"She wears whatever she wants. She doesn't have any powers. If you're really appalled by the lack of variety in colour, I could probably convince Lilian to make you one or two magenta coloured fits. I got a few pink ones upon request."

"It's really not that big of a deal," she said.

"Ya, that's what I thought. The old you never really cared about clothes or fashion like I did." I said, remembering the times before the reality changed. I walked Adelheid to the cafeteria, where a spread of food was waiting for us, just like there always was at mealtime. Another perk of being here was that we didn't have to prepare our food. Lilian did all the hunting, scavenging and cooking. We all followed a primarily plant-based diet, with the odd meat dish once a month. Most days, we ate three times a day. Unless Lexin was upset with us, then he would send us away without dinner or make us train through lunch. The Labs were mostly mainly hospitable, except for the fact that we couldn't leave. Lexin was able to be telepathically connected to all of us, so he knew where we were at all times. Running away was pointless. I tried it once. I didn't get very far. As I explained all this to Adelheid, I watched the light slowly fade from her eyes.

"Can we talk about the crazy schedule Lexin just updated last night?" Silas asked rhetorically, projecting the schedule from his device.

"Why are we doing a 50 km run? Is he trying to kill us?" Silas asked, baffled.

"I'm sorry, what? I don't run." Adelheid exclaimed. We all groaned and then took a closer look at the schedule.

"Trust me, after a week here, you're gonna be jacked. All we do is train, run and eat. We sit in the practice room, and Lexin doesn't let us leave until we show 'an adequate display of our abilities' in Lexin's words." I said.

"He's been increasingly frustrated with us lately. It's like every Begavad expects us to know how to use our powers right when we come of age, but I really don't think it's all that simple," Silas said. "If it were, I'd be parading around in full ice. Just to make CJ feel uncomfortable." Silas gave me a menacing smile. He likes to joke that when he gets good at his powers, he's gonna hold a permanent snow cloud over my head. But like the fire Begavad I am, I do not appreciate the cold. I'd rather be hot and toasty, obviously.

"Wait Silas, don't you run at the speed of light? What's 50km to you?" Adelheid asked.

"He's complaining because he can't stop running until we finish our 50km run, and we do not move at the speed of light." I explained.

"No, y'all move like snails," Silas said. "And every time someone stops or dramatically falls on the floor, Mike I'm looking at you—he adds an extra kilometre," Silas said. The rest of the team and I then continued to explain how our rigorous training usually goes. We also showed Heidi how to use the device to communicate with each other and view our schedules, including training, learning and the rare outings, usually to run in the torturous heat.

"Well, thanks for catching me all up," Adelheid said. "I'm really excited to train with you guys and then die at the end."

The ear-piercing beep that summoned us to the training room sounded, and we all reluctantly made our way over where Lexin was waiting for us in an unsettling manner. Usually, he sits crossed on the floor, and we start with meditation, but today he was swaying back and forth. Lilian was standing next to him simultaneously looking angry and depressed. Poor thing. What did he do to her now?

"Bad things are happening. Really extremely bad things are coming, and we do not have time to play around anymore. Adelheid, I know that technically this would be your first day, but I am sorry. Your first day is going to be tough because we have about a week until our first incoming attack," Lexin said. We had never actually had any real attacks or missions. When I had asked my mother how her time as a Begavad warrior was, she told me it was dull because they trained for threats that never appeared. The idea of having an actual mission was shocking and frightening to me, especially because I know that none of us are ready. "I do not want to lecture you, but in the next five days, I am going to need to see some serious progress. The least amount of sleep a Begavad can have and still be able to function at normal levels is five hours. So from this day on, you will be doing nineteen hours of training, and we will be suspending all theory classes." Everyone started to groan. I looked over at Adelheid, who looked shocked, scared and confused. Silas already looked like he ran the 50km three times over. GG seemed to be on the brink of tears. Mike had dramatically fallen over for no other reason but to show Lexin how much he disagreed with his plan, as he usually displays his protest. I was already dreading getting five hours of sleep because I do enjoy my beauty rest. I rely on it for my sanity.

"Oh, shut it! And Mike, please stand up! If you fall over like that again, we will be doing a 200km run tomorrow and for the unforeseeable future. You know, you really do not have a choice, and you all are favoured. In my division back in the day, I never slept. Do you want to know why?" Lexin asked rhetorically. Every time we complained about training, he used this question to lead into his speech about how he fought in the first world war at our age and then the second world war years later. And that if he is still standing in a couple of centuries, he would no doubt fight in the third world war. All because he is a true Begavad and in his honour, he swore to protect the human kind and blah, blah, blah. To avoid hearing half of his life story for the hundredth time, we all in unison, except for Heidi, replied, 'Sir! Because you fought in the first world war! Sir!' We added in the sirs as a joke to show how obnoxious he was. He never found it funny, but it did help him realize how ridiculous he was being. Of course, we did have it easy. Back at the fortress, we would've had to endure resilience tests. That's where you really get pushed to your limits. So for example, a resilience test for me would be to put me in a sort of ice room, like a freezer and see how long I could survive. Some general examples include chopping of limbs, heads or ripping out hearts. We would be expected to form and reattach those dismembered and displaced parts. Young Begavads actually died from these tests. If you panic and cannot form, you bleed out and die. If you show weakness, you are dismissed from the front lines. Those were warrior Begavads like us, but if you passed, you could go on to be one of the best. We never took the test, we can't form, but our worth is based on the legacy our parents left behind. I'm not sure Lexin would ever go that far, but you never know.

After his speech about the trenches, he'd shut up, wave us off and then leave us to report to Lilian for our suits. After that, I assume he goes to his room or the cafeteria to suck down a few bottles of booze. Adelheid got her suit and as I showed her how it worked, she marvelled at how cool it was. We ran for about two hours and surprisingly, Adelheid was able to keep up. She was almost as fast as Silas. I guess her body remembered the rigorous training.

CHAPTER FOUR

Mars was one of the closest planets to Earth and the only planet the humans had partially explored and considered a plan B once Earth was destroyed. Little did they know, beings already inhabited Mars, and they were the type who would not take kindly to visitors. They didn't even like their own people. The Martians had a similar class structure to Earth, although they only allowed the fittest to live. On Mars, if you weren't born with Begavad powers, you would be cast off the planet. What made Martian Begavads different from Earth Begavads was their ability to teleport and open portals. All Begavad Martians had this ability, except for the powerless ones, of course. After many generations of Martians, their power potency became diluted for unknown reasons. So at the age of fifteen, the Martian children were tested. They were sent through a portal, and if they didn't return, it was said that they were barren and had no powers. Colbalt and Zinc were among the unlucky bunch of Martian children cast off the planet on their reckoning day. Most Martians get lucky and are cast off to a planet like Earth, where their bodies can easily adjust to the change in oxygen levels. In contrast, others end up on Jupiter and wait for a slow, painful death. The Martians were the most disgraced race in the universe. In Earthly Begavad textbooks, they were portrayed as an evil species who cared not for their people but the power alone. At least that's what they taught us, and to never trust a Martian because beings who leave their young to die must be evil, lying, unloyal scum. It wasn't true for all Martians. A group called the Arspens, known as a terrorist group on Mars, believed that casting off the barren was not the correct approach to population control. They were considered terrorists because they defied the Elder Martian council and stole powers from high-class Martians to give to the barren ones, but that is another story, for another day.

Adelheid and her team would soon face Colbalt and Zinc. When Colbalt and Zinc were cast off of Mars they came to Earth around the time Lexin had built Ununseptium Labs and created an immigration asylum for Martians. Long before Lexin started mentoring Begavads, by orders of Queen Klara, he used his Labs as an asylum for fallen Martians. His intentions, at the time, were pure. Lexin believed that all Martians had abilities as it was how their race started. So all he had to do was use science to pull it to the surface. He thought, at first, about kidnapping humans and testing his theory on earthlings first, but then he decided that desperate, depressed and disgraced castaways from Mars were an easier bet. His first lab rats were Colbalt and Zinc. They had volunteered, nay, begged Lexin for the opportunity to be his test subjects. At first, the tests went well. After many weeks of training of the mind, body and soul, Colbalt and Zinc found the ability to create portals, and then they could teleport. Soon after, they developed other abilities. Colbalt had telekinesis and super strength. Zinc developed telepathic and mind control abilities, but with each new milestone came a change in their mentality. What Lexin had feared the most became a reality. Colbalt and Zinc had both become addicted to the power they developed. Much like the Martians they were, once they saw the miracle Lexin performed, they begged for more, and when he refused, Colbalt and Zinc started slaughtering their own. Lexin would wake up every morning to another Martian immigrant dead. For about a week, he had no clue who could've done it and just assumed they had a disease or died naturally. However, one day Colbalt and Zinc admitted to the murders as they realized Lexin wasn't catching on. They told him that if he didn't give them more powers, they would kill every Martian in the asylum. The decision Lexin had to make next was an extremely hard one for his ego. He didn't care much for the lives of the immigrant Martians, but he did care about his tremendous breakthrough with Colbalt and Zinc. He knew he could take them both out within seconds but didn't want his experimentation to go to waste. However, he knew that it was the only way. Lexin had seen the tapestry. He knew that this was not his path, but he had hoped that it would change his fate if he had succeeded, but alas, it had already been sewn into the tapestry. So Lexin trapped Colbalt and Zinc into a Ruby, a small gem that Begavads often use to jail their prisoners. He then went to Mars and delivered them to the Martian authorities where he had hoped Colbalt and Zinc would be detained forever, but of course, in all of his foolishness, he was wrong.

Lilian Herma

"So, what is going to happen to me now?" Lilian asked concerningly. Lexin sighed and rubbed his forehead.

"I am having trouble seeing Lilian. I want to say that this team will protect you, but they are not ready, and the Tapestry Sisters still have the sacred room on lockdown. I need Klara's approval to get in, which we both know is a dead end. So there is no way for me to confirm my theories. We just have to hope, pray even." Lexin said.

"Why can you not protect me? Are you not stronger than them all?" Lilian questioned. Lexin shook his head and let out a long sigh again. He began to pace back and forth in my room.

"It cannot be me, Lilian because the tapestry said so and has said so for years now," he said. I rolled my eyes in frustration. Lexin was obsessed with the tapestry, so much so he let it control his entire life. He would starve himself for years if the tapestry said it to be so. He got one quick glimpse of it years ago, and now he believes his fate is to die at the hands of a child. He believes that he cannot protect me because the tapestry says Adelheid and her team will. But if he can see that they are not ready, and I can see it, the tapestry must be wrong! The tapestry was much the same on Mars, but our loyalty to it was never as strong. Our fate was determined by who we were. If you had powers, you lived, and if you did not, you died. It truly did not matter what the tapestry said, as we mostly used it to unveil prophecies. It was simpler on Mars, but unfortunately, I was cast away from that simplicity.

"So, you would let them take me? Kill me?" I asked angrily.

"Oh, Lilian, please stop your pouting. You must have faith in the tapestry. It tells us our fate, our future, and it says that you will live another 100 years. Now it seems, yes, that the team is not ready, but perhaps in a matter of hours, they might surprise us. If they do not, then maybe it is your fate to die. You have had a long life already, and I do not see what else you could do with it at this point. I have protected you for so long. I raised you like my child, so you should be grateful. You know I abandoned my real children. I lived them out, let them die. I never wanted to be a father. So you should be grateful!" Lexin lectured.

"Yes, you have said that twice now," I said, irritated. Lexin left the room, and I flopped down on my bed. I longed for the days when I was a real Martian, with powers, family and friends. I missed my life. I missed my dad, whom I tried to save. I even missed my rotten mother. Sometimes I kick myself for loving them so much, because I would not be here if I did not. Or maybe Lexin was right. Maybe I was meant to be on Earth. Maybe even, the tapestry said it. No, foolish lies.

CJ (Claire-Joan) Johnson

I met Lexin in the practice room after a five hour practice with the team. Lexin was helping me learn how to open portals and teleport. After my brief and traumatizing trip with Mike, Lexin acquired the ability to open portals and teleport. When I asked him how he suddenly developed these Martian-specific powers, he told me it was none of my business, but I continued to bug him about it. After a few weeks of being in the anti-fortress, he finally told me about the experimentation he had done on himself. I am the only person on my team who has stepped foot into Lexins lab. I've seen what he does in there too. I suppose he told me because he was annoyed by me asking, or maybe because he was fond of me. After I learned how he got his abilities, I told him that it would be better for Lilian to teach me instead of him since I've technically had my powers longer than him. He said that he was a quick learner, wiser than I was and that Lilian had her powers stripped from her, so she couldn't help me. I didn't really care that much. I just wanted to see how he'd react. I secretly liked having private lessons away from the rest of the team. It made me feel special. The only thing keeping me from feeling superior was the fact that Heidi got them too.

"What techniques will you teach me today, Lexin?" I asked as I came in to see him sitting on the floor.

"Today, we meditate," he said with his eyes closed. I sat down in front of him and sighed.

"What is it with you and meditation? I feel like I'm not learning anything from you," I said.

"I am teaching you to be calm and reflective," he said.

"Why do I need to be taught that? I'm sure I already know how," I said.

"Your people are generally impulsive and rash creatures," he said. I frowned.

"That is so rude!" I yelled. I was sure it was racist as well, but at the same time, it seemed inappropriate for a pale individual such as myself to accuse Lexin, what the humans would call Black, of racism, so I didn't say much else.

"It is not. Just an observation of a wise old man from years of experience with the Martian race and culture. This exercise will also help you feel the energy in the room. Remember how that energy feels. Use it to pull the fabric of space apart. That is called portal opening. Now silence." After he said this, we sat in silence for about five minutes until he began to rant. He started how he always did, 'You know what truly bewilders me? It is the fact that...' and then he'd state his grievance. Since Heidi's been back he's observed her behaviour to be 'inadequate for that of an Alpha.' She was 'not meeting the standards for her level and would need to be reprogrammed.' He said that the reality shift had flipped a switch in Heidi that made her into a different person and that he was going to use his last resort to pull the switch out completely and make a new one. I told him that that was a bad idea and a bit extreme. He told me that a threat was coming and he needed to do this. Plus, he had apparently seen it on the tapestry. I wasn't going to argue with the tapestry. He became agitated whenever we did that, so I stopped talking. He said that if I could find a way to get Heidi to focus and rise to our level, then and only then would he consider not using the neuromachine.

CHAPTER FIVE

L exin was right about one thing that day, though. As it came to pass in a matter of hours, after their long 50km run which evidently got stretched to a 100km run due to Mike's theatrics, they were finally all able to form into their element. The details of how they could accomplish this major milestone in their lives are boring and unnecessary to recount in great detail. It is only useful to know that after many hours of screaming and pleading, a new tactic Lexin implemented upon Adelheid's arrival, they finally formed. It seemed that all they needed was a little stress inflicted on them by their mentor to bring out their abilities. Now the only challenge that stood in their way was mastering them enough to be ready for the battle ahead.

Begavads have many sectors in the fortress, just like the human world. Begavads have doctors, scientists, engineers, teachers and warriors of their own. All Begavads are trained to serve and protect humankind, but not all Begavads are warriors. An alpha Begavad team includes a royal, usually heir to the throne and always an Alpha Begavad. Every division had an alpha team, the best, a beta team, the second best and then an army for emergencies. There is a Begavad for each element, composing the team with five members, making the Alpha Begavad the captain. Adelheid was the captain of her team at Ununseptium Labs since she was a royal heir to the throne and possessed all four elements. There were many other warriors in their age group within their division, but they were specifically chosen as the best of the best because of their specialties. They were all special breeds of Begavad, more powerful than their class. Silas was co-captain and second best to Heidi. He was a special breed of Elemente who had the element of not just water but ice, which made him more powerful than the other water Elementes. GG was a Pentaelkay, a rare breed of Elemente who possesses more than one element. She is a class below an Alpha Begavad. She possessed the element of earth and unlike most Begavads, she also possessed the element of water and ice. Mike was special because he was a breed of Elemente with the air element, who could also manipulate the weather—a skill rare air Elementes can possess. CJ was special because she was half Martian, making her more difficult to manipulate telepathically as Earthly Begavad telepaths could only influence those of Earth and the same was true for Martians. CJ could learn to protect herself completely from Earthly telepaths with much discipline. She could have learned, I should say. She never much cared to, though.

After rejoicing in the team's ability to form, Lexin explained the importance of regeneration. The act of forming was used to wield weapons from the elements and regenerate. This is why Begavads often lived forever. There were few ways to kill a Begavad as they were quite resilient. I suppose one could smother or strangle a Begavad to death, but no Begavad would be weak enough to allow that to happen. And if they were, they probably were meant to die anyway. Begavads did not die naturally. There are only two things that could kill a Begavad. The first being a deadly poison native to the garden in the underworld of Hecate, a source of poison that has now been destroyed. Though Hecate may still be growing it, I doubt she will allow anymore out of her sight. The other way was by the sword, but not just any sword, an elemental sword. An air element could never do it because the flow of air has never pierced skin, but fire, ice, a thorny vine or a shard of wood from an earth Elemente, that would do it. To kill a Begavad, you must stab them straight through the heart with an elemental sword, twist the blade for good measure and then slice off the head. You must slice off the head because if you do not, the Begavads could easily regenerate their wounded heart. However, without the connection to the brain, they would die. Everything was explained to Adelheid upon the congratulations of her forming into all four of her elements, quite gracefully, might I add. It left a pit in her stomach knowing that she might soon be killed in such a dreadful manner. 'Tis the fate of an Alpha.'

Mike Larloff

Last week, we all successfully formed into our elements. It was the first time we had seen Lexin smile in a long while. Everything was almost back to normal. CJ and I started hanging out again. She seemed less sad. GG was still quiet and continued to keep to herself, and Adelheid and Silas got their chemistry back. They were starting to get a little too close. According to CJ, she came over to my room every day that week after we hit a peak in our training. She would talk about how Heidi has become obsessed with Silas and doesn't think she's focusing hard enough on training. It sounded like she was jealous. I don't blame her, though. She was talking to me as she paced back and forth across my room, but I was barely listening. She's just repeating herself now. I thought we would be having some fun, but all she's doing is complaining.

"Are you listening to me?" she asked.

"No, babe. I'm not," I said. She huffed and then sat down beside me on the bed. I smiled as I looked at her. CJ's company kept me sane and gave me something to do. If I weren't here, I'd probably just be doing it somewhere else. Likely not the fortress as my behaviour was looked down upon, but I would be out in the human world, living life.

"Don't look at me like that. We're not doing that today. I need your help," she said assertively.

"I'm actually exhausted. I think I might take a nap now."

"You weren't tired when I came in here."

"Yes, well, it turns out… you're boring with your clothes on, so I'm not interested." CJ rolled her eyes.

"Help me with this one thing and then when this is all over, we can finally leave here. We don't have to go back to the fortress. We can run away together to like Europe or something," she said. She gave me a smile and proceeded to explain the situation. This would be the third time she's spoken to me about this and the first time I actually listened. I wish I had listened the first time because what she was saying was so wrong. Lexin had projected his anger and frustration with Adelheid's lack of ability to lead us onto CJ during their private lessons. He has also noticed how infatuated Adelheid has become with Silas and how it's affecting her training. He told CJ that the best thing was to break them apart, and this is where I put my foot down. I could care less about the world's fate or the upcoming attack. I just want to leave this place and live my life. I know that the only way to do that is to get through this training, but I won't let Lexin ruin my best friends' love life over it.

"CJ, what you're saying is crazy. Heidi is your friend, and I'm pretty sure Silas is the only thing keeping her sane. It won't end well if you break them up," I said.

"But why is he the one keeping her sane? Isn't me being here enough?" she asked.

"You're just her friend."

"No, I'm her best friend. She remembers us, but it's like she still doesn't really fully remember us. She only cares about Silas now. She's not taking any of this seriously, and Lexin can't get through to her."

"She's probably just scared. I mean, aren't we all?" CJ rested her head on my shoulder and sighed. I can understand where she's coming from, but breaking them up is not the way. It's hard to find joy in anything being isolated here. If we take the one thing that wakes them up in the morning, we'll be worse off. "What are you proposing?"

"We have to split them up. I'll flirt with Silas, kiss him or something, make her jealous. Maybe it'll light a fire under her ass, and she'll snap out of it," she said, lifting her head from my shoulder. I turned to her and shook my head.

"Or she'll kill you," I argued. She got up and turned her back to me, facing the wall.

"Maybe that's what I have to do, battle her and take her captaincy. That way, I can lead the team and force her to focus," she said excitedly. She turned around to see my reaction.

"You know that you'd have to kill her, right? And she is ten times stronger than you."

"Gee, thanks for all the confidence. And I don't have to kill her. I just have to threaten her enough to deem her unfit so that she will hand over the role to me. She doesn't want it anyway, and I hardly think she has acquired enough knowledge and skill to beat me."

"You saw her run when she got back. All that is muscle memory. She might've taken some time off, but it's clear she hasn't forgotten her training," I said. CJ scoffed and turned away from me again, folding her arms tightly. "CJ, she's your best friend."

"Ya, well, it doesn't feel like that anymore."

If CJ wanted to cut off Adelheid, that is fine, but she's not going to ruin my friendship with Silas. I would give her up in a heartbeat for them.

CJ (Claire-Joan) Johnson

Mike didn't fully understand the problem with Adelheid and her lack of leadership. I went to Mike for help because now Lexin is talking about experimenting on her. At first, I thought he wanted to fix her amnesia, but it sounds like he is trying to make her into a whole different person, and I don't want him to do that. As much as Lexin has helped us in our training, I know that he is not to be fully trusted. My mother and her team were once his trainees, and she told me stories about how evil he was.

She shared how he experimented on Martians, abandoned his flesh and blood and sometimes would lock them in cages when their performance wasn't to his satisfaction. She said it made them stronger, but to be cautious of Lexin. I guess it makes sense why Klara banished him. He is shady. Even though I have been in his lab, and I know about the things he does there, I am still unaware of the extent of his research. I don't want Adelheid to fall into a depression like I did. Still, if she can't focus on mastering abilities so that we can eliminate the upcoming threat, we will never leave here. She will soon face the depressing fate of being trapped in the desert forever. Adelheid likes Silas a whole lot now, but after seeing the same four faces every day for a couple of years here, she will get sick of it. Although it probably won't come to that because if she can't get her head out of the clouds, we will likely all die during battle.

I planned to talk to her tonight. We were all gathering in her room to hang out since Lexin was finally giving us a night of free time, though some of us didn't deserve it. We could all form and do minimal things with our powers. It was just enough to take on one or two people each in a battle, but to become the elite warriors amongst our division, we still had much more to do. I could form a fiery bow and arrow, and a sword. I was currently the best shooter out of all of us. Silas could create an icy sword, eject sharp shards of ice and make gallons of water gush from his arms. GG was able to shoot vines from her hands, and Mike had finally figured out his healing abilities. Adelheid was the only one who still couldn't hit a bullseye during target practice. She could barely swing a sword, and her combat skills were mediocre. She had everything. She had Silas, was captain, is an

Alpha Begavad, and she's just wasting it. If I had everything she had, I would be unstoppable.

I wasn't thinking straight when I walked into Adelheid's room. She was happy to see me for once as she greeted me with a huge smile, but I had just been dwelling on everything that could go wrong, and I had trouble reciprocating the emotion. I thought I had smiled back as I acknowledged her, but then, her smile faded and she looked confused. That's when I noticed I was giving her a dirty look. She didn't say anything. She walked over to her bed and sat next to Silas. We all sat legs crossed in a circle on Adelheid's bed while Mike and Silas argued about which one of them could hold their breath underwater the longest. GG didn't say much, and Adelheid glanced at me cautiously a few times as I stared at her all night, wondering what could be going on in her head. And exactly how I could get her to take things seriously.

"Okay, but if humans are 70% water, then I am 70% a water Elemente. So I could hold my breath underwater just like you," Mike stated.

"I know you know that that's not how that works," Silas replied.

"Well, I did sleep through science so..."

"And that is why you will never be a master inventor such as myself."

"Accurate," Mike exclaimed, and they both laughed.

"Do we have a problem?" Adelheid asked, interrupting Silas and Mike's laughter. Everyone stopped and looked over at me. I simply shook my head and gave a little smile. "Because you've been staring at me all night, and you don't look like you're having fun."

"We shouldn't be having fun. We should be training. Especially you because honestly, Heidi, you kinda suck, at like, everything," I said. Immediately Silas came to Heidi's offence, and Mike turned to me and asked me what I was doing in a whisper. Adelheid waved them off to stop talking and looked me in the eyes.

"CJ, I'm trying, but you know I just got here, and I don't remember how to do any of this," Adelheid said.

"Well, you're not trying hard enough. I don't know how bleak your life was before, but this one isn't all about boys and chilling around. It's about being a Begavad and spending every minute of every day training to be the best. That's what you Alpha's are all about anyway. You don't even deserve to be captain," I said, leaving Adelheid speechless.

"She may not deserve it, but it is her birthright," GG whispered quietly. I snapped my head toward her and gave her a grimace.

"Shut up GG. No one was talking to you," I snarled.

"Hey, watch how you talk to my sister! She's right anyways," Silas yelled.

"CJ, calm down," Mike said as he placed his hand on my shoulder. I looked at him and gradually started heating up, causing the skin on his fingers to sizzle. He winced and quickly jerked his hand away. "CJ, you burned me!"

"Get off my bed, CJ. You'll burn my sheets," Adelheid said.

"How 'bout you make me," I said as the heat from my body started to radiate further. Adelheid formed into a wisp of air, and before I knew it, she was behind me. She tugged on my hair, making me fall to the ground. I fully formed into my element in my anger, and drew my sword of fire. I got up and held it to her neck. "If I kill you, I get to be captain. Then I can lead the team in battle. We'll win, and I can finally leave here."

"You wouldn't kill me. I'm your best friend. You said it yourself," Adelheid said. At this point, Silas, GG and Mike were cautiously standing behind Adelheid. Mike was shaking his head and begging me with his eyes to stop. I looked at Silas, who was shocked at my stance, and GG who just looked scared that I might get her next. I turned my eyes back to Adelheid and continued to point the tip of my blade at her neck.

"I thought we were best friends, but you're different now. You're not the same Heidi, and I don't care for this one. Plus, we both know I could kill you. I mean, you're pretty much useless, so I might as well," I said. With that, Adelheid formed into her fire element and drew a sword.

"See? Look, I can do it too. We don't have to fight. I'll try harder from now on, I promise," Adelheid pleaded.

"Doesn't change the fact that I want to be captain, and the only way to get it is if I kill you, or you could just give it to me," I said. "So, will you step down as captain?" Adelheid took back her skin form and contemplated my offer. She opened her mouth to speak, and then an alarm sounded over the PA system.

"What is that?" Adelheid asked. Suddenly, Lilian busted through the door.

"Quickly children, into the closet!" she yelled. We all shuffled into Adelheid's walk-in closet and sat down on the floor. "There's an intruder in the labs. I am to lock you in here. Do not come out for anyone. Lexin will retrieve you when it is safe."

Lilian closed the door, and I heard her footsteps run off. She slammed Adelheid's room door shut as the alarm continued to sound. It was pitch black in the closet as Lilian had turned off all the lights. Over the alarm, I could hear the sound of Lexin yelling and Lilian screaming.

"That's the biohazard alarm," Silas whispered.

"Do you think there could be a poison exposure?" GG asked.

"Do y'all smell that?" Mike asked. We all shushed him, and then someone turned on the closet light, it was Mike.

"What are you doing?" Silas harshly whispered to Mike. Then Mike pointed to the bottom of the closet door and we all turned our heads to see green smoke entering the closet. Suddenly, I became quite tired. I struggled to keep my eyes open for a few seconds, and then my throat started to sizzle, and everything went black again.

Adelheid Hark

I opened my eyes to a room of darkness. It was neither warm nor cold, and I was wearing all white. Oh no, I'm dead. It must've been that green smoke. It was probably a poisonous gas. If I'm dead, that means my team is probably dead too. I looked around, but all I saw was a void of black.

"Hello!" I screamed.

"Hello." said a female voice.

"God?" I asked.

"God? No, God is male. Don't I sound familiar to you?" The voice asked as a figure came towards me. The dark fog blurred her, and then she came closer and became clear to me.

"Yes, and you look familiar too. You look just like me," I said in awe. It was like she was my twin. She came up to me and smiled warmly.

"That's because I am you, silly," she said.

"How? Where am I? Am I dead?" I asked.

"No, no. You are just within yourself right now. I'm Didi. That's what I call myself, with respect to you being the host. I decided since I love you so much, I'd take your name," she said jokingly, still maintaining the joyful smile on her face. It then occurred to me that I was somehow in my mind, and she was my conscience.

"Not quite," she said. I looked over at her confused. "I can hear what you're thinking, because I am a part of you. Your thoughts are my thoughts. We are one. I'm not a conscience, I am an identity. I'm the human part of you."

"Like a split personality disorder?" I asked.

"Exactly like that," she said.

"But those disorders are caused by trauma. I haven't experienced anything like that," I said.

"The change in your reality was actually pretty traumatic for you. When Alira messed with the tapestry, she unknowingly created me within you. Human Adelheid. I came out to help you with your new human life. It was a lot of fun. I had a whole backstory and a new future planned out for you. I only wish I had more time to publish that book I slaved away on," she said. That seemed to make sense. I don't know all the logistics of being torn away from your reality and being put into a new one with no transition, but I suppose it could be traumatic. That only left the question, if this was so, and I did have another personality, why was I in this dark void? Who was controlling my body? I looked at Didi as I assumed she could hear me, and she smiled with assurance. "When the gas came through the closet door, I watched as it sent all of our friends to sleep. I assumed they were dead which meant we would be going back to our human lives again. I got so excited that I took back the light, and I accidentally kicked you out. I'm only human. So when I took over your body, the gas started to take effect. I nearly passed out, but then Lexin came in to save us and brought us to his lab. After a few hours, we were both pushed back behind this wall, and she appeared."

Didi pointed past me and I turned around to see a girl far off. She was standing in front of what looked like a bright white movie screen. I could make out what she was looking at as I squinted my eyes. It was the medical room. Lexin was there standing beside me, and we were standing in front of a row of beds. My team was in the beds, dead.

"I said I thought they were dead, but they seem to be fine. Just a little sick. Lexin gathered them up after he experimented on us, and they've been in recovery for a few days now." Didi corrected me.

"Could you somehow share your memories with me? Instead of just recounting it all? You can hear my thoughts, but I can't hear yours," I said. She took my hands in hers and nodded. Just like that, it was like seeing my life flash right before my eyes. In a matter of five seconds, I relived my life from when I became human to just a few seconds ago when I asked her to share her thoughts. I hadn't realized that the whole time she was there guiding me through my human life. The only thing that was missing was the life I had before.

"I can't give you those because I wasn't there for that part of your life," she said.

"Who was?" I asked.

"I don't know. Another identity maybe, but I've never seen any others here except for myself and recently, Captain Hark," she said. I turned back to see the other identity standing in front of the screen. She called herself Captain Hark because it was the name that Lexin gave her when he experimented on us. I'm not sure exactly what he did, but according to Didi, there was a lot of screaming, jolts of electricity and overall pain. However, when it was over, this invisible wall came up and Captain Hark had taken the light. I touched the wall and put all my force on it. Unfortunately, my strength wasn't enough, so I tried to form and swung my hand back to summon my sword.

"That won't work here. Even Captain Hark can't use her powers. Only the body can," Didi said. I longed to get my body back. If I was the host, I should control what happens. So, why was she taking over?

"She's just trying to help you. That's why we're here, to help you through life. I helped you stay alive without your abilities when you were Human, and Captain Hark will help you lead your team. I'm an optimist and I trust her. I think that she is doing what's best for us," she said. But she wasn't helping me, she was controlling me. "This isn't what you want, though. You want to be in control. I know it may seem like she's shutting you out of your own life, but I'm an optimist and I believe-"

"You believe she's doing what's best for us. Yes, I heard you the first time. You're starting to sound more like a broken record now. And if you are really here to help me, then why don't you remove this wall?" I asked after cutting her off. If we can't use our powers in this place, how is Captain Hark stopping us from getting through? "As I said, I'm here to help you, but I don't advise you to try and get past this wall. When I was put back here, Captain Hark told me about the mission that Lexin had given to her. She said she would get rid of us if we tried to stop her," she said.

"So can you or can't you get rid of this wall?" I asked. She smiled and turned away. She could, but she knows that if I get past the wall and try to take back the light, Captain Hark might try to get rid of me and then I wouldn't ever get a chance to control my life again because she would take over. I looked back at Didi, who was now sitting on the ground. She looked at me and shrugged, now with a less enthusiastic smile.

"We have to hope that this is the right path for us and trust that Captain Hark knows what she is doing. We just have to be optimistic," she said with a grin. She was already starting to annoy me. I can understand now why Captain Hark trapped her back here. She definitely isn't a threat, she's just a Human. I needed to find a way to get back to the light and take back control. If Captain Hark truly wanted to help me, she would guide me, not put me in the backseat. This wasn't a natural-born identity, stemming from trauma, no doubt, but Lexin's experimentation created Captain Hark. Somehow he found a way to program her into locking parts of me away that didn't benefit the Begavad way. I wasn't Begavad enough for him, so he recreated the Adelheid before the reality change, or a better version of her. Then it occurred to me. If I'm the host and Didi is the human me, then the Begavad me that Lexin didn't create must be here too. If I could find her, maybe together we could take back control!

"That is an interesting idea, but I told you, I haven't seen anyone else here," Didi said.

"Well, have you ever looked?" I asked.

"No, I mostly just lay dormant until you need me. When I was helping you, I stood where Captain Hark was, alone, but then when you came back to the labs, I watched without interference," she said.

"So all I need to do is find a way to get whatever identity was helping me before you, to come out," I exclaimed.

"Ya, but we don't know if such an identity exists, and if they did, we could only bring them out if we knew their motives or if they wanted to," she said. That was it. There must be a part of me that was there before the reality changed, but they don't want to help me because they won't even show themselves. Was my life really that bad that my own self is willing to give it up to some imposter? I turned to find Didi standing right behind me with sympathetic eyes. She put her hand on my shoulder and then pulled me into a hug.

"It's alright. I know it seems like you've been abandoned, but we are only here to help you. If another identity that I don't know about isn't here, it's because you don't need their help. Remember, we just have to be optimistic," she said as she ended our embrace. I turned back to look at Captain Hark. She continued to stare at the screen, or through my eyes, I suppose. I guess this is my life now.

Silas Pushman

I woke up with an excruciating headache. I brought my hand up to my head and winced in pain. The last thing I remember is CJ and Heidi fighting. Wait no, there was a green gas and my throat started sizzling and then I became exhausted and passed out. I sat up from my bed. I looked around and noticed I was in the medical room. Mike was next to me in another bed to my right, and to my left, GG and CJ were in a bed next to Mike. CJ was still passed out, but Mike and GG were awake. Mike turned to me and noticed that I was awake. I still had my hand on my head and looked at him with confusion, but he seemed to be completely fine.

"Here, let me help you with that buddy," he said reaching out to my head. He placed his hand on my forehead, and instantly the ache went away. Mike was getting quite good at using his healing abilities, although a minor headache was nothing. I turned to GG who was sadly lying on her bed staring at the ceiling. Then I faced forward and realized Heidi and Lexin standing at the feet of our beds. Lexin was doing something on his device, and Adelheid was staring past me with her arms crossed. She had a straight face and didn't even look happy to see that I was alive. I waved at her to get her attention. She quickly glanced at me. I smiled, and then she looked back at the wall behind me. It was like she was mad at me or something, but I don't recall doing anything wrong. I turned back to Mike.

"What's going on?" I asked.

"There was an attack a few days ago. Someone released a gallon of concentrated dordaglaje gas into the labs. It nearly killed us, but Lexin managed to save us, but not before they took Lilian," Mike said.

"Where's Lilian?" I asked.

"Don't know. Someone kidnapped her, and Lexin only had time to save us. He said that we had the best chance of getting her back," Mike said.

"Oh good, you are all awake," Lexin said as CJ sprung up from her bed in shock.

"What's going on?" CJ asked.

"Do not be alarmed. Everything is okay now. You have all been in a much-needed sleep for a few days because of exposure to highly concentrated dordaglaje released by Colbalt. This is the threat. Captain Hark will give you all the details. You will have an hour to get dressed and eat breakfast, and then you will report to the training room, where we will continue with our training. The threat is much closer than I anticipated, and we have already lost three days of preparation. However, I have faith in your abilities, and now that your captain is feeling more like herself, I know that she will lead you to a victorious battle," Lexin said. He then gave Heidi the projecting device and left us. With a flick of her wrist, Adelheid gave us a visual of a man.

"This is Colbalt. He's a Martian bounty hunter and ex-barron. He was sent here with Zinc, his sister, also a bounty hunter and ex-barron, to retrieve Lilian, and unfortunately for her they succeeded. Three days ago, he broke into Ununseptium Labs and tried to gas us out. However, he didn't know that as an Alpha Begavad, Lexin and I were immune to the immediate effects of the gas, so he did not anticipate Lexin's attack. Lucky for us, he did not get everything he came for because of this. Colbalt and Zinc were sent here by Martian authorities to collect Lilian for reasons I am not permitted to disclose, but they also had their own agenda. They are willing to make a trade. Lilian, for the undisclosable possession from Lexin," Heidi said in a monotone voice. She was speaking differently, too. Almost like a robot. Mike raised his hand. She acknowledged him and nodded her head.

"What is an 'undisclosable possession'?" he asked.

"I cannot tell you what it is that they want. That is why it is undisclosed," Adelheid said.

"That word completely contradicts itself," Mike said. Adelheid slanted her neck in confusion, squinting her eyes toward him. "Saying undisclosed, meaning 'un' is not, 'dis' is also not and alas 'closed' is not as well. It's just not, not, not, not-- I am very confused."

"Nothing you are saying makes sense, but I assure you the information is accurate," Adelheid assured.

"No, I'm not saying you're lying or anything like that. It's just... Shoot!" Mike exclaimed, slapping his hand to his face. "Sorry, I just healed CJ's headache, and it was a lot. I'm recuperating slowly, but it's like a dordaglaje headache, so I'm just-- I'm kinda messed up... Please uhh-- disregard everything I just said."

"Why can't you tell us? We're your friends, aren't we?" CJ asked.

"I am your captain, and you are my team. You do not need to know Colbalts incentive to defeat him in battle. You just need to follow my orders," Adelheid said. The room went silent. For once CJ was speechless. Even I wasn't sure how to react to the new authoritative Heidi. I guess what CJ had said to her really got through, but now she wasn't even letting us in a little bit. "As per Lexin's orders, you now have fifty-five minutes to get dressed and report to the training room. We will start with a

100km run, then arrow practice, combat and end it off with our first flight lesson. Get to it."

Heidi left the room, and we all looked at each other in amazement at her new demeanour.

"Are you happy now?" I asked CJ. "Heidi is doing exactly what you wanted her to do. I hope you've noticed that you may have gotten the captain you wanted, but now you have one less friend." I got up from my bed and headed to my room. As I walked past the training room, I saw Heidi shooting a fiery arrow. She hit the bullseye twice and then a third time. She had excelled in her training while we were knocked out, and she had forgotten about us.

Lilian Herma

I woke up in a dark, cold cell. As my eyes adjusted to the dim light, I spotted a small spotlight a few meters from my cell. There was a little table and two figures standing over it looking down.

"Hey, Cole. She's awake," one of them whispered. The figures turned to look towards me, and the bigger one started to approach me. As he made it to my confinement, he crouched down and gave me a menacing smile.

"Remember me?" he asked. I squinted and tried to focus on his face. I had a photographic memory, so I was pretty certain I had never seen him before.

"No, should I?" I asked.

"I suppose we never formally met, but I used to live in the labs with you and the Martian refugees, back when it was safe and honourable." I spat in his face. He grimaced at me and whipped it off. "You are the same girl who burnt down the Arspens den. You committed mass genocide."

"How old are you?" I asked curiously. He smiled again and stood up, turning away from my cell.

"You see, when Lexin sent my sister and I back to Mars with our new abilities, we registered as bounty hunters. We were only babies when you killed all those people. Two of them just so happened to be our parents," he explained, pacing back and forth across the perimeter of my cell.

"I am truly sorry. A day never goes by where I do not regret the treachery of my youth. I was doing what I thought was right at the time, and honestly, I had no intention of killing that many beings," I said truthfully. The events of that fateful day have always been a bittersweet memory for me. I single handedly abolished the most prominent terrorist group on Mars, but I also lost my father, the respect of my mother, my best friend and my powers. I lost everything because of a stupid mistake I made when I was fifteen, barely even out of the womb. It was a stupid, though quiet, premeditated, hormone-driven mistake that killed over 500 Martians. Some could argue that the planet is better off, but others would say that it spawned more Arspen followers. Ever since then, bounty hunters have been trying to terminate me. I wish Lexin had let them take me because what is the point of living when you have no power, friends or family?

"Do not be sorry. Our parents were terrorists. I do not disagree with your decision to kill all those Arspens. However, you only made things worse. The Arspens are still the biggest terrorist group on Mars. The only terrorist group really. And ever since your killing spree all those years ago, they have only grown tenfold," he said. I shook my head and fought back my tears. "Oh, do not feel pity upon yourself. It would have happened eventually. Although now, they consume more than 75% of our council and 90% of law enforcement. So, this is where things get really grave for you and your Earthly Begavad."

"What are you saying?" I asked.

"They want the earth. Mars has become overpopulated again, not with live bodies though," he said. My jaw dropped. The Arpsens were truly back and obviously have not forgotten their cruel traditions. "The earth is big enough for the Martians to populate it for the next three centuries and then we will have to colonize Mercury, but that should not be hard. Mercurians are all stupid creatures anyways."

"Why are you telling me this?" I asked. He was going on and giving me his life story, making me feel bad about my poor past life decisions, but I could not help but think he was somehow bragging about it. It did not even seem like he was on the Arspens side. If the Martians came to Earth, they would no doubt kill and probably eat all the humans. The Earthly Begavads would fight against them or repopulate to a different planet to preserve themselves.

"I do not care if the humans live or die. I only want one thing, and Lexin has it. The Arspens sent my sister and me here because the only thing stopping them from colonizing Earth is Lexin and his little team. If I eliminate them, no one will be able to stop the Arspens. Not even the other Earthly Begavads," he says. I am still confused. "But if Lexin gives me what I want, I will leave, and I will not kill your friends."

"The Arspens will just send someone else," I said. His plan did not make sense. And what could he possibly want so bad that he would be willing to go against the Arspens?

"That is likely, but Zinc and I are one of the strongest Martians thanks to Lexin, and if we went back after losing a fight, the Arspens would take further caution. Also, this thing that Lexin has could give me what I need to stop them. Then we both win."

"Thought you did not care about the humans?"

"I do not, but I will be more powerful than ever. I could rule over Mars. I have no desire to stay on this filthy planet. Also, I am vegetarian, so I do not even enjoy the idea of eating any sort of being, especially nasty humans. I hear they taste of dirt," he said. I glanced at Zinc standing by the table quietly observing our conversation. The only question I had left was why they kidnapped me. I could assume it would be to bargain for whatever it is Lexin has that they want so badly. As I contemplated begging them to take me back to Mars instead, Zinc began to approach Colbalt and tapped him on the shoulder.

"Brother, it is time. The half-breed is out of the lab. I can only assume the rest are waiting for us too," she said. Colbalt raised his hand and retrieved the keys to my cell using his telekinesis.

"You are still powerless, are you not?" he asked as he opened my cell. I nodded. "Look at you. Your eyes scream of depression. Even if you did have any power, it does not seem like you have any will to live anyway."

He grabbed my arm, tugged me off from the ground and proceeded to aggressively drag me out of the cell.

"You do not have to be so rough you know. I am cooperating," I said.

"You know, I would apologize, if I actually cared," he said. And with that Zinc opened up a portal to the desert lands, and we all stepped through.

Silas Pushman

Heidi was more focused and determined than ever. It reminded me of how she used to be before the reality shift. The only difference is now Heidi no longer gives me flirty smiles, and it doesn't seem like she enjoys sparing with me like before. She started to scare me as we spared. She never flinched or winced when I hit her with my sword, almost like she couldn't feel it. She kept her eyes on me, and she looked angry the whole time. After she stabbed me up, she decided that we could have a five minute break before Lexin taught us to fly. I already knew how to fly. I didn't have wings like the others or the ability to form into wind like Mike and Heidi did. Instead, I had to use my telekinesis to lift myself up. I had already mastered it. So instead, I took it upon myself to figure out what was going on with Heidi. Judging by her performance so far, she doesn't seem to need the practice.

"Hey, Heidi, Can we talk?" I asked as I tapped her arm to get her attention. She turned and looked at my hand that had just grazed her arm and looked at me sternly.

"You feel hurt. You healed yourself very quickly. Well done. I apologize, but I cannot go any easier on you. That was me barely trying," she explained.

"No, I don't care about the sparring or the very aggressive stabbing for half an hour, but anyways… Can we talk about us?" I asked.

"The team does seem very tense. I know a great team building exercise, but I will require explosives and mud. A lot of mud," she said.

"Um no-- I don't even know what you are referring to… I mean you and me," I said.

"What makes you think there is a you and me?" She asked, still giving me a stern look. I was shocked by this. Before the reality shift, we were most definitely on our way to being engaged. I had given her a promise ring, and we both said 'I love you,' which is a big step for a Begavad. I had almost worked up the courage to ask her mother for permission, and then it happened. When we got her back, I knew things would be different. Yet it seemed we were getting our chemistry back naturally, even with the lack of her memory and the idea of the Silas she wrote about in her book. Everything was going well, and I was willing to wait forever to get back what we had before the time shift, but now she's acting like we were never together at all.

"Heidi, you're my girlfriend, but now you treat me like everyone else. I'm not asking for any special treatment, but you're being so cold," I explained. She didn't seem to care. I was looking into her eyes, and I couldn't see any emotion. It was like looking at a brick wall.

"You will address me as Captain Hark. Whatever we had before is over. I have no recollection of it anyway," she said. Then she turned around and walked away. I stood there for a second in awe until Mike came to me.

"What did you do?" he asked. I looked at him, still shocked at what just happened.

"I have no clue, but there is definitely something wrong with her," I said. "I mean, did you hear what she just said to me? I think we just broke up."

"That sucks. CJ and I kind of broke up too. She wanted to break you two up, so I chose you buddy, and your happiness."

"Thanks Mike, but Heidi and I aren't like you and CJ. Heidi and I love each other. You and CJ… well, you and CJ do what you do."

"That's true. And I think I know what is going on. CJ told me about Lexin being impatient with Heidi's progress and that he was gonna fix her somehow," Mike explained.

"How would he do that?"

"He has some kind of brain machine. It can make you forget things, or it can put stuff in your head that was never there before," Mike said.

"He wouldn't do that," I said. Mike shrugged his shoulders.

"I think he would. Mother always told us to be cautious of Lexin. He's shady, remember? He wasn't even allowed to reside in the fortress. That's why we had to come here. Only untrustworthy Begavad are banned from the fortress," Mike said. I continued to watch Adelheid as she spoke to Lexin. She stood up straight in a robotic and unnatural way and had no expression on her face. She nodded and walked like a machine. Mike was right. He probably did do something to her.

GG Pushman

After every hour of training, the team seemed to get better and better. We were all motivated by Adelheid's new personality, but also scared and confused at the same time. One after another, we would take turns battling her, and one after the other, she would knock us on our butts. I was scared for the battle ahead, but knowing that she had so much more control than she did a few days ago gave me confidence that I might survive. As I flew around in circles with the rest of the team, I daydreamed about my life when I finally got to leave Ununseptium Labs. My dream is to become a doctor, specifically a neuroscientist. In the fortress, we don't really have specializations. Most Begavads in the medical field in the fortress are healers, so they don't have to learn much since they have their powers. I am not a healer, but I truly enjoy the human teachings of neurology. I hope that when I get out of here, I could go to a real school and learn more about it.

"Get your head out of the clouds, GG! Focus!" Adelheid barked at me as she flew past. Or Captain Hark, as she now instructed us to call her. Yes, everything was a bit different now. Adelheid was definitely more ready for battle than ever, but she was a completely different person now. I know I am not the only one who has wondered what happened to her the three days we were asleep.

After two more laps Adelheid finally descended to the ground. Lexin stood at the bottom and waited for us to join him.

"It is time. You must meet Colbalt and Zinc at these coordinates now. I am sending them to your captain. CJ, you will open a portal to wherever Adelheid instructs you to," Lexin said as we huddled around Adelheid. She turned to CJ and whispered something in her ear. CJ then nodded and looked to Lexin.

"I don't get it. Why can't you come with us? Aren't you the most powerful person here?" she asked.

"If I go with you, there will be no one here to guard the merchandise that Colbalt wants. Also, the tapestry says that you must all be the ones to defeat Colbalt. If I interfere, no doubt something worse will happen," Lexin replied. CJ shrugged and opened a portal. As we walked through, I felt the humid desert sun reflect on my skin. It was such a horrible day to pick a fight. But then again, any day would be a horrid one to throw down when you are in the desert. We all stood in a line waiting for someone to appear out of the dusty winds, until finally, we spotted three faint figures. This was it. The moment we had been training for. This could be the very battle that determines whether we live or die. I mean, five against two are pretty good odds. So perhaps we're not screwed.

CHAPTER SIX

B egavads and Humans are in many ways alike, although we hate to admit it. We are a society that started out with the purest intentions—to use our power to help, protect and serve the Humans above all. However, it didn't take long for the Begavad society to become corrupt, just as the Humans were, by the evil that governed our world and created our abilities. The Humans were greedy, selfish, and weak. Begavads strived to be strong, selfless and perfect in every way. But at the end of the day, we are just another version of a human—a stronger, immortal version. Though we strive for perfection, we could never be. Just like Humans, we are selfish and greedy. As it came to pass, many Begavads felt that because we had so much power, and could easily rule over the Humans, we should do just that. It was only Harkolin and her family line that kept this from happening. It was Begavad law that every issue should be settled with a vote. Each of the four first Alpha Begavad got one vote. Harkolin Hark's vote, being the very first Begavad, was worth triple the other four Alpha Begavad leaders. When they split off to different regions of the Earth, Harkolin's family line continued to reign supreme above all the other first Alpha Begavads. The Harks vote continued to be weighed triple than the others. When the matter of ruling the Humans first came up several centuries ago, Harkolin's vote settled the matter. Harkolin was a good Begavad. It is a shame that her kin threatened the world's fate. It tarnished the Hark name. This idea of Begavads ruling over Humans never went away, and when Klara became Queen, it was brought up again. At this point, the Begavad society was entirely corrupt. Harkolin's kin, Klara Hark was at the centre of it all. It was because of her and the corruption from many other Begavads that a prophecy was created. When the prophecy was made, the tapestry sisters witnessed the change in the tapestry. It wasn't a subtle change like the soft wave-like motion the tapestry usually makes when the future is being altered just a bit. It was a profound change that knocked Avlo, one of the tapestry sisters, the one who sews, off her feet and onto the ground as she sewed the tapestry. When they saw this, they immediately reported it to Klara as she was head of the Begavad council. It was protocol for considerable changes in the tapestry to be reported to her, but Klara didn't seem to care. At least that is what it looked like to the sisters, but really, this made Klara happy because she knew that because of this prophecy, the Begavads' time to rule over the Humans would soon come. Alira had seen the prophecy and what she perceived as the horrible end of the Humans. She had seen it being carried out by Harolina. For a while, her kidnapping Harolina and taking her to another planet helped. Still, once the prophecy was set in the tapestry, it could not be changed as Alira had hoped and the fulfillment of the prophecy simply got passed to Adelheid. As the tapestry sisters say, "So it is seen, so it shall be sewn, so we shall protect."

CJ (Claire-Joan) Johnson

We waited twenty minutes in the hot sun before Colbalt, Zinc, and Lilian finally came within our view. I stood to the right of Heidi, and Mike stood beside me. Silas stood to the left of Heidi, and GG beside him. Before we stepped through the portal, I was feeling confident, but I started to feel scared as I saw them approaching. Colbalt was a tall, buff man with the ability of telekinesis and ice, like Silas. Zinc was a short, skinny woman. She was a telepath and possessed the ability to shapeshift. I could feel her combing through my mind. She was struggling. I was only half Martian. My father, who disappeared after my birth, was a Martian. I had less advantage in battle against Zinc because she could partially read my mind. That was the only thing keeping me safe from her full telepathic power. As they finally stopped a couple of meters from us, I grabbed Mike's hand for comfort. He quickly yanked his hand away and gave me an annoyed look. I think he was upset. Everyone was upset with me now. Adelheid came back colder than ever and everyone blamed it on me. Well, they'll be thanking me when we don't die. Imagine if we had loosey-goosey, head-in-the-clouds Heidi captaining our team. We would lose. A team is only as strong as its weakest member. And three days ago, that was Heidi. Now it's back to GG, but we can always count on Silas to watch over his little sister.

"Give us Lilian, and we won't kill you!" Adelheid screamed to Colbalt, who had Lilian draped up by the back of her shirt. Her hands were tied together with a thick rope, which would've been easy for her to get out of had she had her powers, but unfortunately, Lilian was useless when it came to her own defence. He laughed and smiled at Heidi.

"Give me the Dodaroite!" he yelled back. Dodaroite, translated to 'Kill Root' in English. I vaguely remembered learning about this in class back at the fortress. It was the Martian equivalent for what we called dordaglaje. It's an awful poison that could end the life of any Begavad. A flower made from pure evil, death, hate and treachery, naturally grown in the gardens of Hecate. A Swedish Begavad was somehow able to retrieve it from Hecate and nearly died doing so. Since then, the European division has had access to a small supply of this lethal weapon. Some say they sent out teams whose sole purpose was to find soil fertile enough to grow more of the plant, even though the Harks made it a law that no one should ever use the poison. That must've been why we got gassed. Colbalt must've gotten hold of the Dodaroite before Lexin caught him. He probably just wants more.

"We don't have it. It doesn't belong to you, so you will not have it. I don't want to kill you, Colbalt, but I will," Adelheid said.

"The feeling is mutual," Colbalt replied. He turned to Zinc and nodded. She smiled and stared me straight in the eyes.

"She can't control you can she?" Mike asks.

"I don't think so," I answered.

"Mike, retrieve Lilian. Silas, help him. GG, stick with me. We're going to take out Cobalt. CJ, don't let Zinc get past you. The labs aren't too far back. Stand ground here and take her down. The faster we win, the faster we get to go back home. Go!" Heidi exclaimed. I drew my fiery bow just as Mike formed into a gust of wind and moved towards Lilian. Adelheid drew a fiery sword and ran towards Colbalt, but GG stood there confused and distraught.

"GG, you can't just stand there. Heidi gave you orders!" Silas yelled as he formed into his ice element. GG looked at him perplexed like a deer in headlights. Suddenly, Colbalt pushed Lilian towards an open portal as Heidi lunged towards him. Silas grunted and standing by GG's side, he used his telekinesis to catch Lilian before she fell through to who knows where. "Stand behind me if you're not gonna fight then!"

I looked at Zinc, who continued to stare at me. Heidi continued to battle Colbalt. She sliced every one of his limbs off, but he quickly grew them back. I wondered how she might win against him. I figured she might only be stalling as I saw her put a ruby in her pocket before we left the fortress. She was never planning on killing them at all. She was only going to trap them in a ruby and add them to Lexin's collection of villainous prisoners. For Humans, rubies were beautiful rare artifacts. For Begavads, they were holding cells for wrongdoers. At the fortress there are shelves and shelves of rubies holding imposters, killers and Begavad residents who have committed treason. Lexin even had his little collection in his lab. I'm the only one who's seen it. After dismembering Colbalt for the fourth time, Heidi looked back at me.

"CJ! Just shoot her!" Heidi screamed.

"But she's not moving!" I yelled back.

"Just do it!" she screamed. I brought my hand back and got ready to release, but I suddenly started to feel a sharp pain coursing through my whole body, and I was unable to move. I glanced at

Heidi, who was now approaching me angrily. Mike had Lilian and brought her back over to where Silas, GG and I were standing.

"Why aren't you moving?" Heidi asked angrily.

"I can't. I don't know what's happening, but I literally can't move my body!" I said, perplexed.

"Colbalt jumped through a portal. He just left Zinc here, and she's not doing anything. We should leave before he comes back," Mike suggested.

"Colbalt knows where the labs are. If we don't capture him now he will just return to the labs. And Zinc is doing something. She's controlling CJ," Heidi said.

"I thought you said she couldn't control you," Mike said irritatingly.

"I said I thought she couldn't. I didn't think she was strong enough," I said.

"What you mean is YOU weren't strong enough. You should've never let her get into your head like that," Heidi scolded. "Anyway, we can't leave until Colbalt gets back. He could come from anywhere, so everyone keep an eye out."

"Heidi watch out!" Silas screamed. I heard a thud behind me and then another. Suddenly, Zinc looked scared and Mike appeared in front of her. She was sucked into the ruby within two seconds, and I was finally released from my freeze. I let my bow go and turned around to find Silas shielding Adelheid on the ground. He picked up the arrow that landed nearly a centimetre away from my feet.

"Dodaroite," he exclaimed, still leaning over Heidi. Heidi looked at him, shocked and relieved. She looked at the arrow, and then him, then the arrow and then me and then the arrow again. Finally, she looked at Silas as if she was about to cry.

"Silas?" She said confusingly. Her voice this time was not monotone and robotic but soft and a little bit shaky. For a second she looked like she had seen something terrible. Then her worried face quickly turned back into a stern glance and she pushed Silas off of her. "Get off of me!"

She got up from the ground and dusted herself off, walking towards Mike as he approached her with the ruby, trapping Colbalt and Zinc. Silas got up and froze the arrow in a thick layer of glass. He looked at me confused, and I returned the look. What had just happened? We were all confused.

"Good work, Mike. GG, do better next time. CJ, do the bare minimum and open a portal back to the Lab now!" Adelheid exclaimed angrily. I opened up a portal avoiding eye contact with Heidi. I have never felt more embarrassed.

Silas Pushman

Mike had gone to retrieve Lilian from falling into a portal. Heidi was going head to head with Cobalt, while I made sure Lilian wasn't sucked through the portal Cobalt had opened before he commenced an attack on Heidi. She was winning the fight, taking no blows. Meanwhile, CJ was standing there doing absolutely nothing, despite Heidi giving her orders to terminate Zinc. I was hoping Mike would hurry and grab Lilian already as I now had to concentrate on steadily holding a grown woman with my telekinesis while watching over my unprepared, scared little sister. During practice, she did just fine, but it seemed now she was experiencing performance anxiety. I couldn't be too mad. After all, she was my little sister. Mike had finally caught Lilian, and Cobalt had disappeared. Mike and Lilian quickly ran back towards us. CJ was still standing in the same stance, towards Zinc with her bow up. Ridiculous. All this talk about her deserving to be Captain while barely contributing to the fight. I looked back at GG, who was trembling with fear and had tears in her eyes. I told her not to cry and then focused on Heidi approaching us. I hated yelling at my sister. I knew she wasn't ready to be a part of a team, but I couldn't bear to leave her alone in the fortress. We were orphans, and though Mike's mother was always good to us, I was still the only real family GG had.

"What you mean is *you* weren't strong enough, you should've never let her get into your head like that," Heidi scolded toward CJ. "Anyways, we can't leave until Colbalt gets back. He could come from anywhere so everyone keep an eye out."

Heidi stepped towards me and took a ruby out of her pocket.

"CJ can't be trusted. She knows I have the ruby and Zinc has access to her mind. Give this to Mike. Tell him to form, then strike Cobalt when he appears and trap him in the ruby," Heidi whispered in my ear. For a moment, her warm gentil body leaned up against mine, and it reminded me of when she used to be more welcoming. She whispered in my ear and every few words her soft lips would graze my ear, reminding me of everything we were before. She was authoritative, taking charge and coming up with smart ideas to win the day. I liked that about her before, but now she is cold. For some reason, she did not want me anymore. I met her eyes and nodded and for a second she didn't look so mean. I then turned to Mike, handed him the ruby and whispered the same instructions she had just given me. I stepped over to GG and gave her a look of relief.

"It's going to be okay. You will do better next time," I assured her. She gave me a small smile and nodded. I faced Heidi, watching behind her as she faced me, looking off in the distance. Suddenly Cobalt emerged from a few feet behind Heidi and CJ. He drew his bow and shot an arrow just as Mike invisibly swooped over and struck him in the neck. Cobalt fell to the ground just as I knocked Heidi down landing right behind CJ. I looked to my side as I lay on top of Heidi. An arrow was just inches away from CJ's feet with its head coated in poison. I smelled it and immediately recognized its scent.

"Dodaroite," I said, showing Heidi the arrow, still leaning over her. I sat up and showed it to the rest of the team as they were in awe of Cobalt's boldness. Zinc had disappeared into the Ruby, and CJ was released from her grasp. Heidi looked at me, and for a minute, I could see her again. She had her mouth wide open like she was trying to say something, and her eyes were starting to water. She looked at the arrow, then me, then the arrow and then CJ, and then the arrow again.

"Silas?" She said confusingly. I continued to look into her eyes as she maintained a speechless and amazed expression. She looked the same way she did when we first sparred together just after the team had learned to fully form. She was relearning how to spar and she accidentally cut off my arm. I remember how she felt so terrible all day even after I showed her how simple it was to reattach dismembered limbs just by forming. She constantly reminded me how sorry she was and had that same worried look when she asked me over and over if I was sure it wasn't going to get infected, despite there being any indication that my arm had ever been unattached before. I remember laughing at her worry and concern and reminding her that we were indestructible. The only thing that could hurt us was Dordaglaje or Dodaroite, as the Martians call it. I had overheard Lexin speaking to Heidi before practice started. The undisclosed item that Cobalt wanted was the Dordaglaje. He had broken into the Lab the night we got knocked out and he had almost gotten away with a gaseous vile of it, but then Lexin caught him and he decided to use it on us instead. Lexin had lots of it stored in his lab—gaseous types and liquid. Cobalt was only able to escape with a sample of the liquid poison that he must've used to coat the head of the arrow.

I remembered all this as I gazed into Heidi's sorry eyes, just before they turned mean again and she pushed me off her.

"Get off of me!" I rolled onto the ground minding the dangerously poisonous arrow still in my hand. She was being icy again, but that was my thing. I got up and encased the arrow in a thick layer of ice. I had no reason to think that this was any of CJ's doing. As I glanced over at her worried and perplexed, she shared my emotions.

"Good work Mike. GG, do better next time. CJ, do the bare minimum and open a portal back to the Lab now!" Adelheid exclaimed angrily. She neglected to review my stellar performance, and even acknowledged GG for doing nothing. I suppose now she was going to go back to ignoring me. I have to fix this. I can't go another day with Heidi playing the Ice Queen.

We stepped through the portal and made it back to Ununseptium Labs all in one piece. I looked at Heidi who after handing off the ruby to Lexin, turned to look at me with a blank stare. She stared at me like this for a minute. And just as I was starting to lose hope for our relationship, she smiled at me and gave me a kiss, as if everything was back to the way it used to be. Not Heidi before the battle, but the one I knew from the very beginning.

Adelheid Hark

For just a second, it seemed I gained back control and was back behind the wall listening to Didi preach about optimism for the hundredth time. It killed me to watch myself break up with Silas. I could hear everything he was saying. I could even hear everything he was thinking in his mind, but I just couldn't reach him. Now, more than ever, I yearned for the ability to remember my old self. To remember how to be a leader like Captain Hark and love Silas the way I know I did before. The battle was over, and Didi was right. Captain Hark helped lead them to victory, but she also ruined my relationship with Silas. I stood and watched as they stood around waiting for Cobalt. I leaned on the wall and cried out for Silas, knowing it would do no good, but somehow suddenly, for just a second, I had the light. And there he was, Silas, lying right before my eyes. I couldn't muster up anything else but his name and just like that, Captain Hark pushed me back past the wall.

"I told you not to interfere. You'll be lucky if she doesn't kill you now," Didi said. I turned to her and snarled. I pondered at this moment and many others. If it was possible to hate a part of yourself so passionately for being nothing but kind, yet irritating. When I turned to look back at Captain Hark, we were back at the Labs and she was facing me.

"We won. I did it," she said.

"We did it," I said. She shook her head.

"I know you think I am the bad guy, but I am not. And in the end, I did it. You almost ruined everything, but I still did it," she said. Then suddenly, we were both at the light. "I am giving you back control now."

"You plan on taking over again?" I asked.

"Only if you need me too. Do not slack off, and I will not interfere, but I would be wary of that boy. He will never let you live up to your greatest potential," she said. And just like that, Captain Hark disappeared right before I could even ask her if she knew my old self. I turned to my right to see Didi standing beside me.

"Ugh, she let you out too?" I groaned. She smiled at me and shook her head.

"I'm not Didi," she said.

"Who are you then?" I asked.

"Allow me to share this with you," she said as she grabbed my hands.

CHAPTER SEVEN

Though Begavads could live on for several centuries, Begavad royals must continue to pass on the throne to the next generation. Usually this occurs when the Queen has a child. When that child comes of age, finds a suitor and bears children of her own, they are crowned as queen. In Arlo's case, she did not take the throne after she had Adelheid and the other one that shall not be named. She had not been the first to recognize the hypocrisy and toxicity of the royal hierarchy, but she was the first to deny the crown in her family because of it. She was appalled by her mother's callous behaviour toward her kidnapped child. She had no interest in continuing the trend. When the reality shifted, Arlo was thankful because she finally got a chance to raise Adelheid away from the influence of the fortress. The news of how Adelheid and her team defeated Cobalt and Zinc travelled back to the fortress within hours. Also recounted was that Adelheid was back to herself. Arlo had been inspired by Adelheid every day since she accepted her fate after the reality shift. It was this inspiration that led Arlo to finally accept the crown. The coronation process was a boring outdated event that is rather best left unrecounted. So, I will give you a summary of what occurs. The soon-to-be Queen walks down the aisle. Behind her follows her nominated right hand. The right hand is usually always a woman, and the soon-to-be Queen must nominate someone, usually a close friend or a loyal and trusted teammate upon her swearing-in. The Queen will either accept or decline the soon-to-be Queen's right hand. If she accepts, they would be sworn-in too. The princess and her right hand, if she has chosen one at the time, will follow behind them. There's a whole set of vows to recite which are not necessary for anyone to know as I recount this tale, and then everyone bows to the new Queen. There's a party, usually where the former Queen invites suitors from other divisions to be presented to the princess. Then there is a dinner with the immediate family of the Queen and the family of her right hand and remaining team members. The coronation day is an all-day celebration. It's fun to imagine, but when you're the one being fitted into a glove-sized corset, it starts to feel like more of a sacrifice.

Silas Pushman

"I remember. I remember everything," Heidi said as she gazed into my eyes. I can't believe it. Just like that, she was off and then suddenly she was back on again. Like, she was really back. She turned around and faced the rest of the team. "I remember everyone. Mike, GG… CJ. I get it. I know why you were mad. Part of me was too."

She walked over to CJ and hugged her.

"I'm so glad you're back because everyone was really starting to hate me for giving you such a hard time," CJ said jokingly.

We all laughed and then Heidi turned to Lexin. He glanced at Heidi and then walked away. She looked back at me with a big smile and kissed me again. Everything was back to normal. Like, really back to normal. Who knows, maybe next we'll actually get to go home.

Lexin Lambois

I added Cobalt and Zinc's ruby to my collection. Despite the many complications the children had done well for their first mission. Then I sensed a presence in my lab, and I turned around. It was Adelheid. I proceeded with caution. I had heard what she said to Silas and the others as they returned to the lab, and I knew she was not the same person who left the anti-fortress before the mission.

"When my mother told me we were being sent to you, she made it a point to let me know that I was the most powerful Begavad. After you, of course. I've been trying to get into your head for a while. It doesn't help that you locked me out of my own," she said, staring at me menacingly.

"Who am I speaking to?" I asked as she took a step towards me.

"You should already know," she said, taking another step towards me.

"Well I cannot read your mind," I replied, stepping back. I would be lying if I said I was not intimidated by her. I knew of all her personalities. I put Captain Hark in her mind to monitor them all, but I could see that Captain Hark was not speaking with me. She would never approach me in such a threatening manner as Adelheid did now. I also could not read her mind. She was powerful. That was true, but not more powerful than me. Although she was powerful enough to block me out.

"Then use some sense," she said, stepping towards me. "I'm just a little upset that you tried to replace me with Captain Hark. I thought we were on the same page."

"I am sorry you feel that way," I said unsympathetically. She took two more steps towards me, and I backed up into my desk. She rolled her eyes and got right up in front of me. "What are you doing?"

Adelheid pulled out an arrow and held the head to my neck.

"You're not sorry. Lucky for you, Captain Hark is surprisingly very cooperative. However, I am vengeful!" she exclaimed. I looked at the arrow and smelt the poisonous Dordaglaje on the head.

"You cannot kill me. The tapestry does not want this. Not now," I plead.

"I don't hail to the tapestry. Unfortunately, there's not enough of this substance to kill you, but it will bring you a lot of pain and suffering until I finally do kill you, and by then the tapestry will be true," she said. I tried to move my arms to push her away, but I was paralysed. I tried to form into water to flow away, but I could not do anything. "You should never underestimate me, Lexin. Your reign is over."

She dragged the arrow across the side of my neck while maintaining intense eye contact with me, and when she was done, she dropped it on the ground, stepped back and smiled. I winced in pain as I felt the poison enter my bloodstream. The effects were already making me feel weak. I fell to my knees as

I watched her walk towards the exit of my lab, but she stopped just as she reached the door.

"Oh, and it's Lady Hark, by the way, but you already knew that," she said. She then left my lab and closed the door.

I spent three hours recuperating after giving myself a shot of adrenaline. It was Begavad adrenaline, so it would only last for a couple of days, then I would need more. I was not sure of the exact day when Adelheid would finish what she started, but I had made my peace with it since the tapestry says it must be so. I was ready to go. I know that I should have left this earth decades ago, but I was not prepared. I lived a life of selfishness, greed and an insatiable desire for power, but I was never truly happy. I only wish she did not make me suffer because I have already been suffering for many, many, many years. Now I am tired. Now, I am ready.

Adelheid Hark

After I made sure Lexin was aware that I knew what he had done, I met Silas outside of the labs. We had a special place a couple of miles away. It was an unnatural anomaly—an underground cave with glowing water and shimmery black rocks. No one else knew about it except for us. We sat on the edge of the dip and let our feet soak in the water as we sat side by side in silence for a while. I could tell that he had a lot on his mind and so much to say. I tried to never read the minds of my friends, family, or anyone really unless it was completely necessary, but I didn't need to read their minds to feel the vibes. That came naturally. I looked at him as he looked at the glowing water in suspense. Finally, I nudged him on the shoulder and he looked up at me. I smiled and he smiled back uneasily.

"What's wrong?" I asked.

"You know what's wrong," he replied. I shook my head. He always assumes I invade his mental privacy, but I don't.

"No, tell me what's wrong," I demanded. He took his feet out of the water and turned to face me, now crossing his legs.

"I love that you remember everything now, and you feel more like yourself but..." he paused and looked away uncomfortably. I think I know where this is going. "The way you were acting before, that wasn't amnesia or the reality shift. That was something else. I know Lexin did something to you."

"Lexin..." I said. How should I go about this? Do I tell him about my personalities? It might change everything. Before the reality shift I, Lady Hark, didn't even know I was a personality. If I told him what Lexin did, he would get upset. And if I told him about my other personalities, he would think I was crazy. Maybe that's what I wanted. I minded what Captain Hark had said to Adelheid before we took control, but I'm not sure I was ready to accept my fate. "He taught me how to be a perfect Begavad. I was for a few days, but it's hard to be perfect when you're not capable of perfection. Everyone was relying on me. I think that's why I shut everyone out because I was focusing so hard on being something I'm not. When you saved me from getting hit by that arrow earlier, I realized that I would never be the perfect Begavad. And that's okay because I don't need to be perfect, despite what Lexin said."

Silas nodded and gave out a sigh of relief.

"Mike had me thinking that Lexin messed with your brain, and I believed him because you were being so cold. Then you broke up with me," he said.

"Lexin told me to do that, but obviously, I changed my mind. You make me better every day, and if I ever wanted to be anything near perfect, I'd need you by my side to do it," I said. He smiled at me, and I smiled back. It's better this way. What he doesn't know won't hurt him. I have control over the body now, and it seems that all other personalities concerned have a mutual agreement to cooperate in the best interest of Adelheid. This was in the best interest of Adelheid.

After the sun went down, Silas fell asleep. I didn't want to leave him alone or ask him to run back to the labs half awake, so I stayed with him, and I suppose I fell asleep too.

Arlo Hark

Today was my big day. My coronation day. The day I would finally become Queen after twenty years of hesitation. I finally decided to take the throne, and I was already regretting it.

"Besides the fact that killing people is most definitely not God's will, this corset—mother! Well it is not my will! It's the same size as my arm! How do you expect me to wrap my arm skin around my waist? How?" I screamed to my mother as I swung the door open to my fitting room and charged towards the chaise where Cece was sitting. I had almost forgotten the insane rules I had to follow as Queen until I took a crash course last night. The outdated rules and regulations were ridiculous, and when I tried to reason with her, she attempted to pass it off as 'God's will.' This is the exact reason I never took the throne in the first place. The royal families think they can do anything. Kill anyone, put stupid and immoral mandates in place and as long as they say it's 'God's will,' everyone will bow down and believe them. This was also the reason I had to take the throne now, so I could clean things up before Heidi got it.

"No one is asking you to wrap the skin of your arms around your waist!" My mother screamed back. I sat down on the chaise and turned my back to her as I crossed my arms. I could burst into flames right now. "Arlo, this gown has been passed down from generation to generation. Our head Queen, leader and the very first Begavad, Harkolin wore it, and the corset is mandatory so you can fit in the dress."

"Why can't you just fit it to my size? We all know that it's been altered before. Harkolin definitely did not wear a dress with a veil of gold on her coronation," I said, still turning my back to her. The dress was beautiful. It was a dark purple, fitted waist, open at the front bottom with a long gold veil that hung behind me. But it was a size zero, and I, as the humans say, have thick bones.

"It was God's will for Harkolin to have a veil of gold actually," my mother said.

"Harkolin was a peasant! She didn't even have copper to her name! She knew many days of starvation until she got her abilities. That's the only reason why she could ever fit in that dress!" I said, turning my head to scream at my mother. She didn't even look tired. She opened her mouth to speak again, but I got up and snatched the dress from her before she could. "Never mind then! You won't give up. I'll wear the dress, but don't be surprised when I drop dead upon walking down the aisle."

"I suppose we should get to it then," Cece said as she stuck out her hands for me to hand her the dress. My mother had left the room, and I rolled my eyes and went over to lay down on the couch.

"Just give me a minute. I want to remember how to breathe for just one last time," I said sarcastically. I sat down on the chaise and as I was about to lay down, I realized CJ and Heidi were being fitted for their dresses right in front of me. I got up and looked at Cece. "Why didn't you tell me that my daughter was here?"

"I thought you knew," Cece said confused.

"How could I know things if you don't tell them to me?!" I screamed.

"You're a telepath, aren't you? Or has that changed since I've been gone?" Cece asked sarcastically. I turned to Heidi and CJ and smiled.

"Hello girls I'm so sorry that you had to see that," I apologized as they continued to be fitted for their dresses.

"It's okay. I enjoyed the show. Like, where's the popcorn! I'm just kidding. I'm nervous. Can you tell I'm nervous?" CJ asked.

"Of course, it is natural to be nervous when you have to sit in front of a crowd. Usually, only the Queen would be presented with her right-hand woman. Still, I figured since it was technically Adelheid's first time being presented as heir since she learned how to walk. You two were so close that I'd have you be presented as her right-hand woman as well," I explained. "If that's still what you both want."

"Yes. CJ is my best friend. I want her to be by my side forever." Heidi said with a smile.

"And, of course, the feeling is mutual, but I'm actually not nervous about the coronation. I just haven't seen my mother in so long. I barely know what to say," CJ said.

"Oh, that's right. It has been a while since you two have been together. Well I'm sure you had some time to catch up while I was disagreeing with the Queen," I said.

"No. Actually, we didn't really talk," she said awkwardly.

"Well, there will be plenty of time for catching up after the coronation when we have the celebratory dinner," I said. I turned around and walked over to CeCe who minded my corset and turned her back to the girls.

"Why haven't you spoken to your daughter? You haven't seen her since she was ten!" I scolded.

"I didn't know what to say. I knew CJ would ask about her father, if I opened my mouth. And if she asked about her father, I would have to tell her that I still hadn't found him. Which is not all a lie in reality," she said as she ironed out the kinks in my gown.

"You can't keep lying to her. You have to tell her the truth." I said.

"If I told her the truth, I'd have to tell her that her father is dead. If she knew that he was dead, she'd ask how, and if I told her how, she'd ask who," she said, holding up the gown and staring at it. She put it down on the table and opened up my corset. "She is so much like her father. And knowing the person he was, she would want revenge. But it's not like she'd have to look far. She's already living in the labs with that Martian. Not to mention that if I truly told her the truth, the whole truth, she would hate him for being who he was. Most of all, she would hate me for not telling her. It's just been too long, and we're already estranged. I don't need her to hate me too."

"It's not too late, and she won't hate you. She longs to have a relationship with you. I can see it in her eyes, and most of all, I can feel it in her heart. I may have also read like a quarter of her mind, and I can see it there too. She won't hate you. She could never hate you. Just promise me you'll tell her because if you don't, she'll find out some other way and then it will really be too late." I begged. She turned to me and nodded.

"I promise. Now enough of that. Let's get this corset on," she said, wrapping it around my waist.

"We don't have to do the corset. It's truly not necessary," I pleaded.

"No, no, no, I am not getting in trouble with your mother. I need to be in her good graces if I want to be approved as your right hand," she said as she started to tighten the corset.

"My MoThEr! Loves you. She EvEn lOvEs YoU... uhhh... more than me!" I said as I struggled to breathe.

"Don't know why, but I suppose I should be thankful to be accepted by the Queen, since my whole family comes from a long line of screw-ups. Even Clan was a screw-up, and he wasn't even blood," she said as she tugged on the strings.

"Do you miss him?" I asked as she finished off the corset.

"I try not to. CJ's father lied to me multiple times. I can't say that I'm glad he's dead, but I definitely don't want him to be here anymore," she said as I turned around to face her.

"I just never understood why Lilian would kill her father?" I asked, referring to Clan, Cece's late husband and father to CJ and Lilian.

"Maybe she found out that he left her and her mother to be with another woman. Or maybe she found out he was a terrorist. There are a plethora of reasons why one would want to kill their father," she retorted. I shook my head.

"It just doesn't seem like Lilian. She was never vengeful," I said.

"Martians are cruel beings. Lilian has been reformed. Yes, by Lexin's fake comportment, but I wouldn't be surprised if she were nothing less like her father. Evil. Just because she showed us kindness in our youth doesn't mean she was kind in hers," she said. I put on my gown, and she spun me around. "Beautiful, just absolutely stunning. Alright, it looks like the girls are ready. We should inform your mother. The sooner we start, the sooner we get to breathe."

CJ (Ceceilia-Jane) Johnson

The ceremony had gone well. To my surprise, former Queen Klara accepted me as Arlos' right-hand. I guess she was right about Klara liking me, for whatever reason. We were now observing the part of the day where we stood around with our alcoholic drinks and socialized with visiting divisions. Selected Begavads from all over the world came to see Arlo's long-awaited coronation. They had also come to offer up their royal sons for Adelheid's hand. For royal Begavads who bear males, it is important to seek out another Alpha Begavad female to make Queen. An Alpha Begavad Queen can have a lower class Begavad as King. However, an Alpha Begavad male must always have a female Alpha Begavad as Queen and nothing else. It was a part of the same outdated and stupid rules that Arlo was hoping to change. I had been avoiding CJ all day, even though Arlo, or the Queen, I should now say, pleaded with me to tell her the truth about her father. I had reasoned with myself that if I didn't end up running into her then, it was probably the universe telling me not to tell her anything, but then I did. She approached me and gave me an awkward smile. Before she could say anything, I grabbed her hand and took her to my room. I sat her down on the couch and looked her in the eyes.

"I want you to know that it was never my intention to abandon you," I said.

"You didn't abandon me. I was really young when you left, but I remember that you said it was because you went to find my father. I've always admired you for not giving up on him. I wish I could find true love like you did," she said.

"I haven't been completely honest with you. What your father and I had wasn't true love. I thought I loved him at first. I gave myself away to him, but then I realized he had lied to me. That's why I've been gone for so long because I was ashamed that I let him do that to me. Then when I found out the truth, I was too ashamed to tell you or anyone. Only the Queen, your captain's mother, knows the truth," I said.

"What are you saying?" she asked. I took a deep breath and told her everything.

The truth was that I never truly knew who Clan was. As a youngster, I never followed the rules. The pledge of abstinence was my favourite rule to break. So when I went on my first mission to Mars with Arlo, I didn't hesitate to sample the Martian men. After we finished our mission, a simple kill order, an Earthly Begavad had been caught scouting out soil for a deadly and illegal plant on Mars. Arlo and I stayed a few days. When I had met Clan, he was the head authority of the Martian law enforcement team. He had helped Arlo and I track down the Earthly Begavad. He was also an Alpha Begavad. By Martian terms, I had never been with an Alpha before. I was intrigued by him, but it wasn't just his sex appeal, but his mind and his heart. I felt that I loved him, so I extended my stay on Mars. It was our last mission anyway since Arlo was starting to settle down with Jake. So I thought I might do the same. After about a week, I convinced Clan to come back to Earth with me. It was very easy. After about a month, Arlo and I shared the news that we were pregnant, and we shared a room in the fortress' hospitality ward. CJ was to be born a month or two after Adelheid.

It wasn't until after I had given birth that a problem arised. My mother had no idea I was even pregnant, but she forced me to marry Clan when she found out. Of course, I was not opposed to this idea so, I proposed it to him. He told me that he couldn't marry me because he was already married to someone else. When Martians marry, they take an immortal bond. It prevents them from bonding with anyone else. So when I came to him with excitement in inheriting the Martian tradition of an immortal bond, he had to tell me the truth as to why I couldn't take part. He was stupid. He was a cheater, but he wasn't a coward. I told him to leave me alone and go back to Mars, but he wouldn't leave. He insisted on staying until CJ was old enough so he could pass on his immortality. As an Alpha Begavad, he would be able to hand down his immortality without the result of death. I only knew he was decent because he was still willing to do this. I then thought, maybe he just made a mistake. Maybe the woman he was bonded to wasn't the one, and I was. Maybe, I would learn to accept and forgive him for lying to me.

Well, he still went back to Mars. I told him to give me some space and return in a year or two, but he never did. I knew that he still loved me and wanted to be with me. I also knew that there was no way he would abandon his daughter without passing down his immortality to her. So I knew that something must've gone terribly wrong. So when CJ was ten, I left her to find him. It wasn't just for me. I also needed him to keep the promise he made me and pass his immortality to CJ as she would soon come of age. The first place I looked was Mars, obviously. I went down to the law enforcement head-quarters and asked for him. They told me that he had died in a mass attack where the Arspens, a Martian terrorist group, held their meetings. I was shocked. I had no idea he was a terrorist. I learned at the fortress and from Lexin that all Martians were evil-spirited beings, but he didn't seem that way. From what I gathered, the Arspens were only considered terrorists on Mars because they stole powers from other Martians to give to barren Martians, but the Martians who they stole from would be killed in the process. It was no better than the way Martians killed the barren on their planet when they came of age. I then learned that Lilian was the one who killed over 500 Martian Arspens who had been gathered to celebrate the birthday of their Arspen leader. I was even more shocked by this when I learned that Lilian was his daughter. I had met Lilian once or twice long after I left the anti-fortress. She resided there with Lexin, but she never spoke of her past. So, I had no idea her father was my lover.

I could've lived with knowing that Clan was a terrorist, sadist and overall rotten to the core. I had been with worse. But what truly made me hate him was that he indirectly killed one of my best friends. I couldn't face my team or CJ after finding out what happened to Clan. I could live with the shame, but I wasn't ready to be scolded by everyone else. So, I stopped in Australia on my way back from Mars. There were few Begavads there because there was no Australian division. I planned to stay there for a week or two, but I never left. It was only about a week ago that Arlo had finally convinced me to return for her coronation. Unfortunately, I never returned to watch my best friend and her husband Gene-Gwen and Parko Pushman, not only give up their immortality to their two children, but also to my own. It killed them, and it was partially my fault. I had taken my chances with an Alpha Martian Begavad, gotten pregnant, abandoned my child, let members of my team die taking responsibility for my child and left two children orphaned. I couldn't possibly go home after that. Arlo had found me months after my return from Mars and I told her everything. We kept in touch, and I praised her for not forcing me to return. She never looked down on me or hated me for what I did to our friends. That's why I felt I owed it to her to be there for her coronation and pledge my life and never-ending loyalty to her as her right-hand woman.

After I told CJ everything she had to know about her father, I expected her to yell at me or walk away without a word. But instead, she hugged me. She just hugged me, and I was so confused. I asked her what she was doing and she said that she forgave me. I never felt more solid. Maybe CJ wasn't anything like Clan. Maybe she was kind, strong and well rounded. Maybe, I didn't have to worry at all. Maybe, I shouldn't have stayed away. All I knew now was that I wasn't going back to Australia any time soon.

GG Pushman

After the ceremony, Silas and I decided to pay a visit to our mother in the Garden of ME's—a sacred Garden growing with the trees of our ancestors, reserved for Pentaelkays with the Earth element. When they died, they took their true form of a tree. ME stood for Mother Earth as all Begavads with the Earth element were endowed with such motherly and sacred aspects. We hadn't seen her since we left for the anti-fortress, five years before she passed. Silas was ten when she passed, and I was only eight. I didn't completely understand the rituals of our people at the time, and I didn't take her passing too well. As I grew older, I began to understand why she had to go, but there were still pieces missing. Begavads have created a hierarchy like Humans, but they have made it with a justified meaning, unlike Humans. Humans create a ranking based on the bias of who they presume most powerful. Even though all Humans are more or less equally as powerful and none are powerful enough to claim superiority. However, the Begavad hierarchy is solely based on power. If you're an Alpha Begavad, you are immediately at the top of the food chain because they are rare. Thus they are royalty. They are allowed to pass on their mortality multiple times before it takes a toll on their body. Pentelkays are just under Alpha Begavads. They are allowed to pass on their immortality twice at most before they slowly weed away.

Elementes are at the bottom, where they can only pass on their immortality once, and then they die immediately.

My mother was a Pentaelkay, as most earth-wielding Begavads are. But for some reason, after she passed her immortality onto me, she died shortly after. Although it was traumatizing and unexpected for me, I was glad I could finally visit her again in the garden. It was quiet and I heard only birds and buzzing bees. While most of the fortress has been built underground, the ME garden is amongst the Human society in a secluded area that was bought by Begavads many decades ago for this purpose. Not many humans pass by here, and if they do, they walk by quietly and have no clue what it is they are encountering. The last time we visited mother, I was thirteen and it was just before we left for the anti-fortress. We sat by the tree and leaned against her trunk and Silas explained the Begavad circle of life to me. This time, we sat by the tree and leaned against her trunk in silence, until Queen Arlo came to greet us.

"I came here every week to pay my respects. You have no idea what a hero your mother was," Queen Arlo said. She began to descend in between us. Silas stopped her and took off his coat.

"Oh, please, my Queen. Do not sit on these grounds, or else you shall truly ruin your royal gown. Please, allow me to offer you my coat," Silas said as he placed his coat under her. She smiled at him and nodded.

"Such a good young man you are and handsome too. This is why I have no fears for you to become my daughter's husband," she said. Silas and I shared a glance. He blushed and looked at the Queen. "I can tell that you love her. I don't even have to ask."

"It's true," he assured her. Arlo took off her ring. It was a gold band with beautiful lavender stone upon it. She gave it to Silas as he awed at its beauty. "For me, my Queen?"

"Yes, I give this to you. And I'm sure you know why. You have my blessing to pass on this family heirloom and propose to my Adelheid whenever you should feel ready to do so," she said. She got up and brushed off her behind. Silas swiftly stood up soon after and bowed before her. As he bowed, he glanced at me. I took the signal to get up and bow as well, so I did.

"Thank you, my Queen," Silas said.

"While I appreciate the respect, please, do not bow to me. You are practically children of my own now, and Hark's bow for no one," she said. Arlo smiled gracefully and walked back to the gate where her porter was waiting. "I suppose you need a way back to the fortress? I don't see your porter."

We both nodded and ran up to her, following her through the portal. When we got back to the fortress, we wandered the halls until we came across the others in an empty hallway.

"We should do that every month, like Queen Arlo does," I said to Silas as we began to approach the others. He looked at me and nodded.

"If Lexin gives us freedom, then we shall," he said. Queen Arlo called mother a hero. It made me wonder what heroic act she did that was superior to the rest of her team that earned her that title. Must've been something huge to have an Alpha Begavad mourn her every week. Often, as the Human royals would, the Alpha's would look down on us like we were all equally peasant folk.

Mike Larloff

I had just enjoyed a lovely conversation with my mother and three girls she wanted me to choose for marriage. I told my mother that I had no interest in getting married so soon and already had a girlfriend, prompting the girls to walk away and leaving my mother to scold me.

"You cannot in any circumstances marry CJ," she exclaimed angrily after I told her that CJ and I were seeing each other.

"I never said I wanted to marry her, but now that you don't want me to, I sort of want to," I said, looking off into the crowd.

"No! No! CJ is a bad seed. You'll see if you choose to stay with her," she said. I shook my head.

"Whatever, Mom," I said as I rolled my eyes. As I gazed upon the crowd, I spotted Heidi talking to four guys. She was subtly making eye contact with me. Then I heard her voice in my head. 'Yo! Mike, save me please!' she pleaded.

"Are you listening to me, boy! Do not marry that tramp! I have plenty of others…"

"I'm sorry, mother, but I have to go now," I said cutting her off, and I walked over to Adelheid. I smiled at the guys who were all speaking at once about how great they were.

"It is well known that *my* family is rich. We own five countries in the Netherlands."

"Oh, please! Every Begavad division has its riches. We have acquired wealth over the centuries. It would be shameful if we did not. My family is known for our Alpha genetics, whereas the Friedls have had peasant children."

"Blasphemy! We have a pure Alpha Begavad line!"

"We do not, but we have no fear in admitting such because we are very honest. I thought I heard that your family was known for witchcraft."

"Nonsense! Whoever told you that should be sentenced to death!"

"Oh my…" Adelheid said, putting down her head.

"Gentlemen, I am so sorry to interrupt. I'm Princess Adelheid's faithful servant, and I do have to steal her away for just a few minutes for royal business. You know, the usual."

"You don't seem like a royal servant," the snobby royal in the middle exclaimed.

"Why thank you, but we really must be going now," I said leading Adelheid away. We pushed through the crowd and found our way to a hallway where no one was congregating.

"Thank you so much. These royal boys won't give me a break, and the way that they're talking sounds like we stepped through a portal into the medieval era," she said looking around to assure the coast was clear.

"You forget it is the most respectful way to speak to an Alpha royal, don't ask me why, though. I don't pay attention in class. How'd you do that back there, by the way?" I asked. "You spoke to me with your brain."

"I'm a telepath. Remember, the only problem is I still have to work on my range or else I would've called someone else, like Silas or CJ. Where is CJ anyways? She's supposed to be my right-hand but she disappeared right after the ceremony."

"Well, that's not very right handly." I joked. "But you know, you could always count on me right? I *am* your friend."

"Are you my friend? It always seemed like you were more of Silas' friend then mine," she said. I opened my mouth to speak, then Silas and GG appeared and began to walk towards us. "Where have you two been?"

"We went to visit the garden of ME's," Silas replied.

"Finally got to see mom's tree. She's the tallest one there, you know. Even taller than Alira," GG mentioned.

"I always thought the tallest tree was the Begavad with the most power," I hypothesized. Adelheid shrugged.

"Maybe the Hark family isn't the most powerful after all," she joked. Then out of nowhere, CJ appeared dazzled and pale. Behind her, Lilian followed.

"We need to have a team meeting, now," she said irritatingly.

"Well, coincidently, the teams are all here. Just wait for Lilian to catch up," Adelheid said. CJ looked back and frowned. Adelheid's watch started to beep, and she looked at it concerningly.

"Actually, it's about Lilian," CJ mumbled. I looked at her confused, and she met my eyes with distress.

"Hold that thought. There's a problem at the lab," she said as she projected the warning signal. "Seems like there's a toxic gas leak. I'll go check it out."

"You want me to come with you?" Please?" CJ asked desperately. Adelheid shook her head and closed the projection.

"It could be lethal. I'll go air out the labs and be back right before the dinner," Adelheid said.

"Oh! Hail! Princess Adelheid I have been searching for you for hours! Wait, wait there!" a Scottish prince yelled as he ran down the hallway towards us.

"Oh, woe is me," Adelheid said sarcastically. She turned to Silas. "Hey you. Don't be too intimidated. These suitors mean nothing to me. All they have to offer is money I don't need and old English I can hardly understand."

"I know. It just sucks that you have to leave so early. This is your celebration too," Silas replied.

"Oh you poor old fool… are you going to miss me?" Adelheid sarcastically asked as she ripped the seams off her dress.

"Not anymore then I should," he replied jokingly. She handed him the bottom parts of her dress and took out her suit.

"Well don't you worry, I'll be back soon," she said, handing me the corset. "And I would very much like to escape that," Adelheid said, pointing to the boy, as she stood before us wearing nothing but an off-white bodysuit.

"You better run then," I said. She nodded, activated her suit, and started to run in the opposite direction. Looking back once or twice, Adelheid turned the corner just as the Scottish boy reached us. He stopped and gasped, struggling to catch his breath.

"Say you, will she be returning?" he asked.

CHAPTER EIGHT

For Humans, death is forever. If they subscribe to the right God, they would likely get a second chance, but if they do not, they would likely be burned in the eternal flames of hell. However, for Begavads, death is never the end. There is always a chance to regain your soul. When a Begavad dies, they are offered another chance, which usually takes quite a while due to their everlasting life span. Their soul leaves their body and they are grounded by an ME. This grounding ritual is unnecessary, but like Humans, Begavads have created unnecessary traditions and practices that have nothing to do with their religion. After their soul leaves their body, they are taken to purgatory, where they sit and wait for a trial date. Begavads are given the chance to stand amongst the Lords of Olympus and plead for another chance or a spot in heaven. Zeus and Hades sat before the dead and fought over who would get your soul and whoever got tired first would forfeit their chances. If Zeus won, you had a free ticket to heaven or back to Earth. But if Hades won, there was usually an ulterior motive to allowing you back to Earth. It never used to be this way, though. Zeus and Hades used to be both civil Lords working only for the one true God, but then Hades became too involved with the inner workings of hell. And though he won't admit it, he became a friend to the evil one himself. The wait in purgatory could be hours, days, months or even years until you get a trial date. Still, until then, you had to wait in a void of white with nothing but your thoughts.

GG Pushman

You were the only one who knew my truth and accepted me for everything I was. I never expected you to be my first kiss. I know you didn't expect it either. I remember it fondly. Others would've made a scene or condemned me, but you didn't, and that's why I never forgot the compassion and kindness you showed me. We were messing around with some elemental combinations in the classroom that would probably be toxic to the average man. You had shown me how to roll a spliff the day before, and I had prepared one for you to examine. You said it looked good but the only way to truly test if it was satisfactory was to smoke it. So, we did. I made some good weed, we both got high, and I kissed you. You stepped back and knocked a beaker over with your hand in the shock. I felt so bad, guilty, and ashamed. I immediately apologized and bent down to clean up the mess. You told me not to apologize and followed suit. You got a shard of glass stuck in your hand, we didn't know how to fully form yet, so I took it out and patched you up using methods I learned from books about healing science. It's an art they no longer taught ever since they decided to leave the healing duties to natural-born healers. You told me that I didn't need the healer ability, and how I was a pretty good 'doctor' as the Humans would call it. Then you said that what I had just done was technically sexual assault but that you would allow it because you were my friend, and you accepted me either way. However, I had to ask permission next time. You'd probably politely decline but it was the right steps to take when kissing someone. I laughed because I knew you were mostly being comical, but I also felt relieved that I had at least one person I didn't have to hide around.

Silas used to tell me that death wasn't the end, but my mother died, and she never returned. This makes me think that the tales of Olympus are false. Your death allowed me to show my strengths, as I singularly rebuilt the labs after your fiery demise, but it does not bring me any joy that you are gone. I will mourn for you, and I will miss you. This team won't be the same without you, and I suppose my secret dies with you.

Mike Larloff

I don't think you ever knew how much I cared for you. You couldn't have because I never honestly told you. I busied myself with other girls thinking I could ignore my feelings for you, but how can I? You were always around, and I was always reminded of how unattainable you were. As I stand in front of your grave with the others, I reflect. I know everyone is thinking it, but I should have been there with you. Maybe if I had, I could have healed you and perhaps you wouldn't have died. You were my first crush, but I suppose, now that you are gone, you won't be my last.

CJ (Claire-Joan) Johnson

How do I put into words the pain I feel now that you're gone? I can only imagine that everyone else wishes they could have been there in your last moments. Most probably because they think they could circumvent your last moments. But I feel even worse because I know I should have not taken 'no' for an answer when you said you'd go alone. I was your right-hand woman. I should have opened a portal for you to the lab and back. Then perhaps this would've never happened. Lexin said it was the Dordaglaje that got you, but when we returned to the labs everything was burnt to ash and the grounds were sunken in, leaving nothing but a pit of darkness. You left everything behind—your betrothed, your throne, your captaincy. I hated that it brought me joy that now I could have it all. I can only have it because you're gone. I would be lying if I said that I didn't often wish for this, but my heart was almost always overrun with jealousy. You were perfect, pretty, smart, strong, and you had everything. You had the attention of every boy in the entire land. You had the throne in your midst and the power in your veins. More power than I could ever imagine. I wanted everything you had, but not like this. It's only in your death that I can admit I feel this way.

Silas Pushman

I think I could be in shock. Everything happened so fast. One moment I was visiting my mother with GG, then I was accepting your family heirloom ring, and getting the Queen's blessing. I spoke to you in the hallway of the fortress with the others, and then you left. And now you're dead. I once told GG that death was not the end. I believed what I said at the time, but my mother never came back, and she should have never died, just like you should have never died. Instead, my mother left GG and I orphaned. We moved in with Mike and his mother, but it was never the same. Adelheid, you left me too soon and to make it worse, you took a chunk of my heart with you. I have my sister, my brother, but I don't have you. And you're not coming back. If there's anything I learned from being an orphan, it is that your loved ones never come back. We stood by your grave for hours, reflecting in the hot sun in silence. We didn't even have anything to bury. Your body and the rest of the lab was burned to ash. Even CJ's clothes didn't survive the fire, as it was mixed with poison. It was more than just a raging flame. It was a poisonous mixture that would have decimated any soul. The celebration ended shortly after you left. The Queen then began searching for you around the fortress. I assured her that you'd be back soon, but you never came back. I ran over there as quickly as I could, and I saw the plot on fire. I readily jumped in with my icy form, but the fire burned and sizzled my skin unnaturally. Lexin pulled me out of the flames and told me to stop. He held me down and made me watch as the flames devoured the lab with you inside them.

"Alright, we should go back now. Everyone, as I taught you," Lexin said, breaking the silence. Everyone held out a ball of their element in the palm of their hands. GG threw a blob of water into her grave, then Mike a ball of lightning. CJ threw in a ball of fire, and I put in a ball of ice. GG then covered her grave with dirt and kneeled to ground her.

"I don't even see the point. We're burying air," I said, turning to Lexin.

"This is the way we do things. Also, GG must learn. When there is a body to bury, one day, she will need this skill. It is her earthly duty," Lexin said.

"Where were you Lexin?" I asked. He shrugged towards me. CJ turned around to face Lexin also.

"You were supposed to be at the labs during the coronation, so where did you go?" CJ asked.

"It is none of your concern," Lexin said looking off to the distance. Mike turned around angrily as the air stopped moving.

"Well, it is a concern because if you were here, she wouldn't be dead," Mike said.

"Did I do it right?" GG asked meekly. I turned to look at her, teary-eyed looking up at the rest of us. I quickly turned away to compose myself. I couldn't cry. I couldn't be weak like she was. Heidi wouldn't want that. I focused my anger on Lexin to fight back the tears.

"Just forget it, GG it's pointless anyways," I said. "You know it's your fault, right?"

"And why would you suggest that?" Lexin asked.

"It's not a suggestion Lexin. It's a fact. Heidi sent her last transmission right before she died. So whoever triggered the gas warning was there for Lilian," CJ said. "I know what you did. Lilian, and I know Lexin knows what you did too. She deserves to die! And so do you!"

"Stop! That is enough!" Lexin barked. He turned away from us and shuddered. "Open the portal. Just take us back."

CJ reluctantly opened a portal back to the labs. GG stepped through, then Mike, then Lilian and Lexin.

"Silas," she said.

"I think I need to take a walk," I said without turning to her.

"Okay, I understand," she said. Then she left, and I was alone in the desert with nothing but vast sandy land and a grave filled with dirt. I ran back to the fortress and told the Queen what had happened. She told me that she already knew, that she could feel it.

"It feels the same as when her sister passed," she said.

"Sister?" I asked. I didn't know Heidi had a sister.

"Never mind," she said. I disregarded her comment anyway, not like it mattered. I tried to offer her back the ring, but she closed my hands and shook her head.

"Keep it. It's the only thing you have left of her," she said.

"But what about you, my Queen?" I asked. "What do you have to remember her?"

"Nothing, but for me, it is better just to forget. I've had much practice with such already," she said. "Now go, be with your sister. She'll need you more than ever now."

I didn't know whether Heidi would return or not, but keeping the ring didn't help in comforting me. Instead, it only made things feel worse. Like a reminder of what I almost had, but then lost before I could even try to retrieve it.

I could easily leave, run away somewhere far off. Heidi was gone, so there was no one to captain the team. And Lexin seemed too weak to keep us jailed anyway. Whatever was going on with him, I didn't know and I didn't care. But I went back to the labs, because the Queen told me to and because she believed my sister would need me there. So I did, but every inch of the labs reminded me of her.

Adelheid Hark

I was in another void. It looked like my void except for white, and there was no screen. Perhaps I had changed it but then where was everybody else? I spun around to view my surroundings but saw nothing but white. Then someone appeared, a skinny little man.

"Hello, I am Hermes, Herald to the Lords. Do you know who you are?" he asked. I had heard of Hermes, the Herald of the Lords. In the human world, he, along with the other lords of Olympus, was considered a Greek God, but we Begavads knew the truth of their titles. I then knew where I was. I was not within myself. I was in purgatory. I was dead.

"I'm Adelheid," I said. "Hark."

"Ahhhhh, we have a royal in our midst. We have not seen a Hark here in a while. Is your grandmother still living?" he asked.

"She is." I answered.

"That woman clings to life like gum to a shoe," he said jokingly. He giggled, I didn't laugh. We stood there for a while and stared at each other. I'm sure he came here for something, but now I'm just not sure.

"Is that for me?" I asked, pointing to the scroll in his hand.

"Oh yes, I shall read it to you," he said, opening up the scroll and holding it to his face. "On the noon of June 30, Adelheid Hark was obliterated by a high-density poison. Show flashback here." He stopped and looked at me.

"What?" I asked.

"Do you want me to show flashbacks here?" he asked.

"Of what?" I asked.

"Of how you died," he replied. I thought about it for a second. Do I, the strongest Begavad that used to live, want to see how I was so easily defeated?

"No," I said involuntarily, but I did want to see it. I couldn't even remember how it happened.

"No, she doesn't," someone said as I felt a hand on my shoulder. I turned to see myself standing beside me. She smiled, and now I was perplexed.

"Your consciousness and your soul are here. Your body still lies on Earth, in ashes of course, so do not be afraid if you come across your inner demons," Hermes said.

"Lady Hark?" I asked. Turning to myself, she shook her head. "Captain?"

"We've never met before, but don't worry, I'm here now," she said.

"All right, well, your court date is set for October 25," Hermes said, closing the scroll.

"What! But that is months away!" screamed a familiar tone. I turned to my right to see who I can only assume was Captain Hark.

"I do not make the dates," he said.

"Well, what am I to do until then?" I asked.

"You are a lucky one. You have all these demons to keep you company," Hermes said as he started to walk away.

"They're not demons," I said. Hermes turned and looked me in the eyes.

"Are you sure about that?" Then he disappeared.

"This is ridiculous. The team will fall apart without me," Captain Hark said.

"You mean without us?" Lady Hark corrected.

"Oh shush, you know I do all the work anyway," she corrected.

"Not true, but alas, I haven't the energy to fight you right now because I'm dead. We're dead," Lady Hark said.

"Silas will surely crumble into a crippling depression once he realizes we're gone," Didi added.

"I'm sure he'll be fine. Everything is fine. We're fine." The unknown identity spoke. I looked around to see them all here with me, Captain Hark, annoyed and unhappy, Lady Hark, indifferent, Didi, sad and this unknown identity. I noticed they couldn't hear my thoughts and I couldn't hear theirs.

"You all came with me," I said.

"We had no choice. We are a part of your consciousness. So if you die, we die," Captain Hark said. She came up close to my face and continued to frown. "So please, try not to make this a habit."

"I swear, I didn't do this on purpose. I just wish I knew what happened," I said.

"She knows what happened," Lady Hark said, pointing to the personality beside me. She looked at me and smiled.

"What happened... There is no reason to recount the tragic tale. We're dead now, right? So we all know that, and that is all we need to know. We shall sit here and wait a few months and then hopefully return to Earth. Everything is fine. The team will be fine, everyone will be fine. We are all fine," she said reassuringly.

"I really enjoy your optimism," Didi said joyfully. I rolled my eyes.

"Just tell me. I can handle it," I pleaded.

"Do you think if you could truly handle it we'd all be here?" she asked. She was right. If I was mentally strong enough, I wouldn't need any of them. But I'm not. I suppose this was all a part of the plan. Maybe Lexin saw it in his tapestry. I still had things I had to accomplish back on Earth. This wasn't the end. This can't be the end.

CHAPTER NINE

The Begavad society was built on a Christian foundation with Christian values. However, it became evident that those values have been more or less diluted over time. There is no clear story of how or why we exist. Some say our main purpose is to protect the Earth's timeline. Some say it is to protect the Humans themselves. While others are convinced that we are to rule the Humans and believe in the prophecy of Mordare the Frailslayer, an old legend of an ancient being who would bring the Humans to their end and allow for the rise of the Begavads. No one has the truth, but what we do have are rules. Outdated, misguided rules that have been in place since the beginning of time.

Do not kill any human; as Begavads, we must remember that our power could very well be used for evil. As it was a gift from the very personification of evil himself. Still, God was the one who allowed us to keep this power, so we must follow his will and never kill any one of his children. We do not have the authority to judge them for their sins, and thus any Begavad who kills a Human is sentenced to immediate death.

Never make yourself known to the human race. We stayed underground in areas that were least populated on the Earth, so we did not bother or scare the humans with our presence.

However, if they knew what power we had and what we could do for them, they would likely try to praise us as their God. It would be sinful to proclaim ourselves as God's so we stay away from Humans. We still have gated communities where Begavads who work in human affairs live to provide certain services beneficial to Earthly kind, but we never show our powers to the Humans.

Do not practice witchcraft. Another rule that has been bent. Most Begavads choose not to practice witchcraft because dark magic requires a heavy price with each spell or incantation. Not to mention, there is the selling of your soul to the evilest spirit—however, one particular division, the Timpani's, practice witchcraft. Despite the very clear rule against it. We would persecute them, but 95% of the African Division would be deceased. Executing that many people is just not a priority, especially since their witchcraft only affects themselves.

Maintaining abstinence; as I mentioned, the very roots of the Begavad society are tied to Christian traditions. Maintaining abstinence is strongly encouraged. Marriage to the Begavad is nothing but a signal to God so that children can be born in his name. For the will and protection of his people, I suppose. It was of utmost importance that royal Begavads have children. Every Begavad below them was also encouraged to follow suit to continue growing the Begavad society. Homosexuality was strongly discouraged. It was not a rule in Begavad society that you could not be homosexual, though it was in the Christian scriptures. The Begavad looked at it more practically. Being homosexual did not allow those Begavads to reproduce, so it was frowned upon as it was not productive. Being a Begavad had no room for love. So any type of romantic attraction was meaning-less anyway. Each of the finest Begavad warriors who remained in the anti-fortress had broken at least one of these rules over their lifetime. Or, they were starting to realize that they did not fit the Begavad mold. Yet they still remained the most skilled team of the Begavad society until their succession, of course.

CJ (Claire-Joan) Johnson

Heidi has been dead for several months, and the mood in the labs has shifted. Everyone is either sick, depressed or upset with me. After Heidi died we had a funeral for her, even though there was no body. We were all upset with Lexin for not being there. He never told us where he was, and he refused to admit that it was partially his fault. GG pushed Silas into hibernation after she suggested we watch the tapes. Lexin had years worth of videos of us in the labs. We don't know why he had them, but he did, and they were fun to watch. For a while, it was comforting to see Heidi in the tapes again. It seemed to make Silas feel a little bit better too. Until he pulled the wrong tape. It left a bitter taste in all our mouths. Silas left enraged at GG. He was mad at her for a few days, and just when I thought he had gotten over it, GG and Mike did something that pushed Silas further away from them. I guess Silas had it all bottled up inside, and he decided he was done with us all because since then, Silas has been hibernating in his room. Lexin agreed that the team had truly fallen apart now, and I feared he would do something about it. His solutions are never good.

I accepted defeat and went down to the training room to train. I was shocked to see Lexin there meditating. He usually stayed in his room too. I sat down in front of him, and he opened one eye to acknowledge me.

"I tried getting into the sacred room again... I may or may not be banned," I said and his eyes shot open.

"Why? I explicitly told you not to go there!" he screamed.

"I know. I just wanted to see when she'd be back... because I miss her."

"No, you do not. You lie."

"Of course I do. She's like a sister to me."

"When she comes back, she will take everything away from you, and you want that more than you want her. You did not check the tapestry because you missed her. Instead, you checked it because you need to know how much time you have left to live her life."

"Not like you're not wondering the same thing."

"I am hoping she returns soon so I can put myself out of my misery."

"I'm sorry to hear that."

"No, you are not," he scolded. "Anyway, it does not matter. There is another mission and it is very important. You cannot go alone. We will need to fix Silas, and I will need your assistance."

"No. I'm not doing that to him. I'll take Mike," I said.

"It needs to be a water Elemente. You will be up against the flames."

"I'll take GG then."

"While GG has proven herself useful, you and I both know that she is not ready to go on a level 4 mission. You will take Silas. We will do the procedure tomorrow."

"Fine."

"I know you are reluctant, but I am willing to turn him in your favour."

"What do you mean by that?" I asked.

"Adelheid's death is one thing, but after what GG and Mike did, I doubt he would collaborate with them again. And he never really liked you, did he?" I looked at him angrily. He didn't *not* like me. We just weren't as close. I'm sure it's because he knew I had a crush on him and he didn't reciprocate. "Well, if we do this, I can make it so that you and Heidi's roles are somewhat reversed in his head. I will also assure that he has no memory of GG's admission and her involvement with Mike. I cannot fix your grudge with Mike, however."

"I have no resentment towards Mike. We all know that this is just how he is."

"Well then it is done. Lilian will lure Silas out. All you have to do is meet me in the lab at noon."

I didn't agree with this idea, but I wasn't going to stop it either. Silas would die in his room if we didn't do something soon. Seemed like all we had to gain was a fully functioning team. I'd get a chance to be with Silas romantically, Mike would likely hate me for it, but he'll get over it once he realizes that Silas has forgotten about his encounter with GG. And GG will be thankful that Silas will no longer be disowning her. It should go nicely.

GG Pushman

Almost everything burned in the fire, except for the sub-basement. Lexin had saved many things down there. I suppose he knew something like this would happen. He always knew. He had lab equipment in the sub-basement. Enough to replenish his lab and more, although now he rarely used it. I quarrelled with him for a few days over the usage of his lab for myself, but even in his weakened state, I lost. So I made my lab in my room. I showed my true potential when I helped rebuild the labs with my wood and vines. It seemed more like the real fortress now, with the wooden walls and green vines spiralling all over.

I was in the lab with Mike working on my project. I had already visited the fortress to resign from the team and apply for a mentorship in the inventors ward. I wanted to apply to be a healer, but the Queen said it would be best that I go with invention since there was no one to teach me how to be a healer. "We don't offer courses on medical solutions like that. Healers don't have a rule book or procedures to follow. They simply do what they do because that's what they do," she had said. "I'm sorry, but either stay with the team or choose something else. There are plenty of teaching positions available. If you'd like to train in the invention ward, I'd be happy to recommend you."

I took what I could get. I wasn't too sure I wanted to be a teacher or a mentor like Lexin.

"So basically, you want to find a way to transfer our Begavad abilities onto inanimate objects, like a gun?" Mike asked as he read my paper.

"Well, a gun is just a minor example. I mean, imagine if we could shoot bullets of fire or ice or even wood, I guess," I replied.

"Or wind bullets," Mike exclaimed.

"Exactly, those are especially lethal!" I joked. He laughed. "We can do so much with our elements, but what if we could do more?"

"Ya, I get it. Your hypothesis is bold, borderline fantastical, but maybe we can fix that. See what you did wrong here..." Mike said as he began to correct and expand on my work. He had just agreed to help me with this project. It would be our life's work, but I was a scientist and this is what I wanted to do. Mike was a scientist now too, I suppose. When we were younger, he never seemed committed to our classes. But that all changed after Heidi died. I'm not sure why he suddenly switched his persona. I just knew I liked him better this way. I was thinking about all the different things about him now and all the ways he had matured. I think he had the biggest glow up out of all of us. Now, he was staring at me. Probably waiting for me to agree with him, but I wasn't listening to his hypothesis. Instead, I was busy admiring his growth.

"Totally, that makes so much sense. Good idea," I said.

"I just spent fifteen minutes explaining how hotdogs grew on trees, and that's all I get?" Mike joked.

"Wait really? Did I just applaud you on that? Sorry I wasn't..."

"Paying attention?" he asked.

"Right. My bad." I said.

"No worries. Is there something on your mind?" he asked.

"No, well, kind of. I'm just really grateful that you are willing to work on this with me. It's amazing how far you've come.

How smart you've become. You're wiser too. I've noticed. I like you better now."

"You seemed to like me just fine as I remember it," he said. My eyes widened, and I stared at him in embarrassment. I know he meant it as a joke, but it still reminded me of the shame I felt after that night. "Sorry. I shouldn't have said that."

"It's fine. I shouldn't have come to you."

"But I'm glad that you did. I mean, I'm not happy about what we did, but I'm glad you came to me for help... or whatever that was. I just wish I had gone about it differently, that's all. I would never do that again, not even if you begged me to."

"You didn't like it?" I asked shyly, making minimal eye contact and turning away from him.

"Did you?" he asked. I looked back over to my desk and then turned my chair to face him, and he did the same.

"Maybe I like both," I said.

"It's okay GG. It's okay if you didn't like it." he said, and that made me burst into tears. I couldn't be this way. My brother hated me this way. Mike got up from his chair and held me in his arms. I cried over his shoulder and used his shirt to wipe my tears.

"He disowned me!" I said as I sobbed.

"Silas is in a bad place right now, but he may get over it. I will always be here. I could be your brother," he said awkwardly. And I groaned grossly. "I know. It probably doesn't seem right to take that title now."

I didn't know what else to say. So I just stayed in Mike's arms and cried. He patted my back and told me to let it all out.

He stroked my hair with his hand, and it reminded me of the night we spent together. I didn't shudder at the memory of us, but I liked it better than my current reality. I wanted to like it. I wanted to want him, but I couldn't because I wasn't like him. Mike thinks Silas will get over what we did, but I don't think he will. We hurt him, and though Mike found a way to grow and forgive himself, I never can. This was who I was, and there was nothing I could do about it. Silas was going to hate me forever, and I was going to be alone. Mike says he will stay with me, but eventually, he will find a nice woman and leave me. I won't have him forever. I can't have him forever.

Adelheid Hark

It was an enriching five months in purgatory. The unknown identity, which I later learned was named Ishalo. She constantly reassured me that I was fine, and we were fine, and everything was just fine. Ishalo was weird and anxious, but I felt calm and relaxed around her. It was as if she were holding all the anxiety and worry I might have, so I wouldn't have to deal with it. I also learned a lot about myself. Mostly that I felt weak, knowing I had to rely on all these personalities to keep me afloat. Ishalo's words echoed in my head over and over again. 'Do you think if you could truly handle it we'd all be here,' so one day I snapped.

"Am I just a puppet to you?" I asked. She looked at me perplexed.

"No, of course not. I exist only to serve you, help you, and keep you going," Ishalo replied.

"But without you, without all of you. I'm what?" I asked.

"You are a Begavad," Captain Hark piped in, taking a break from her daily quarrel with Lady Hark.

"You are a strong Alpha woman. We make you stronger, and even without us you could survive. You just needed a little help, that's all. That's not to say we'll be here forever," Lady Hark assured me.

"I've been thinking a lot about that. I'm sure this disorder doesn't work this way with Humans," I suggested. They all nodded.

"I'm sure there are aspects of it that are a bit different," Isha-lo agreed.

"Well that means there could be a cure for me. For us. Begavad technology is much more advanced." I said.

"You don't think you need me?" Ishalo asked. I frowned.

"You are the only one here that has chosen not to share what brought you here. And it's a pretty big deal why you're here." I said.

"You want to know how you died?" she asked. I nodded. It wasn't so much to ask. To desire answers about yourself. I know my personalities were created to help me cope with my trauma, but I only had so much trouble then because I was a child. The reality shift wasn't the first insurgence of a personality split. When I came to know Lady Hark, I realized that. Lady Hark was my first personality, named after the nickname my father gave me. My father, I barely remembered him. He gave his life for me when I was fifteen. Though it was a ritual all Begavad children had to go through, I'm the only one who came back with immortality *and* mental instability from it. The ritual didn't go wrong, it worked perfectly, but the event was scary. The bright light bursting through my fathers heart and snapping onto mine, then watching him disintegrate into nothingness. I don't think I was meant to watch. Most children don't, but I did, and it sent me into a frenzy. I started crying, screaming and throwing myself around the room as my mother begged me to calm down. Then I blacked out. When I woke up, Lady Hark had been created and I had forgotten everything that happened. Lady Hark got me through most of Lexins teachings in the beginning, and Didi got me through Human life. Captain Hark helped me through my first mission. Even though I'm reluctant to thank that imposter for anything, and Ishalo was attempting to get me through death. It's an unnatural thing. When you die, you should just die. There should be peace, not a misty white waiting room and what feels like eternal boredom for a chance to get back out there and live again. I don't want to die, or I didn't want to die. But the next time it happens, I want it to be forever. No waiting room, just dirt, just peace.

"You know, sharing the trauma you were created to protect her from sort of defeats the purpose of your existence," Ishalo said to the others, who looked offended at her criticism. "But if you really want to know so badly, I suppose I could share with you how you died."

Ishalo put out her hands toward me. She was only going to share how I died, no biggie. It's just death. I can handle it. I can totally handle it.

CHAPTER TEN

After a long day of work, Hades and Zeus would take the extra initiative to look through the defendants for the next day's trial, and they would argue and bicker over who would get who. Zeus was sympathetic and wise but was never not easily won over by a sad sob story. At the same time, Hades was sadistic and only allowed Begavads to return to Earth if they made a deal with him. Hades was not the evil one who shall not be named. He was well acquainted with him but was not him, and Zeus was not God. Zeus and Hades were like lords to God and the evil spirit. Hades was lower in power and significance than Zeus, but I am biased, and this is not the point. The point is that when Hades came across Lexin's name on the list, he went into a fit of rage when he saw Zeus sign a claim on him.

"Lexin is mine, mind you!" Hades exclaimed.

"Lexin has redeemed himself. He shall be judged by our higher power. You have no claim over anything when He does." Zeus explained.

"Lexin made a deal with me over 500 years ago. His soul is mine." Hades protested.

"You have got to stop making deals with people," Zeus said, rolling his eyes and continuing to look through the scrolls of the dead. "It is not fair, and it is not the will of God."

"I do not serve your God, and I am not a slave to the other one either."

"But you are. You collect souls, damn people to the underworld and claim yourself as the reaper."

Hades shook his head in disagreement and rolled his eyes. "Lexin is mine," Hades said again.

"Good luck taking him from the Lord's grasp. He has many pounds over you," Zeus said, ending the disagreement. Hades never got to use Lexin the way he thought he would, which was probably for the best. He has used powerful Begavads before and the tasks they complete for him would always damn them. But Lexin didn't need Hades' help to warrant himself a passage to hell. He was already rotten to the core. Surely, he trained one of the strongest Begavads ever to live, but he also had a shady past. The reason for which Klara had banned Lexin was not that he was a royal son of the Lambois family, but a traitor to the Begavad way, and a manipulative being who took advantage of her daughter. Lexin and Arlo, simply put, had something of a love story before Jake. It was not widely known amongst anyone. Not even Adelheid or Jake knew about it. You could count the sum of people who knew of the royal scandal on one hand. Alira knew, Klara, CJ, Arlo's right-hand woman and I, being in present power, knew the scandals of my ancestors. When I sought out this story, I learned that a certain Martian knew too about the truth behind Lexin's banishment and the royal family secret. It was not the first time Arlo had to pretend a child she bore did not exist when Adelheid's twin sister was taken. It had been the second time this had happened to Arlo, but the first time she was more easily swayed to forget her. You could say that Arlo was just as much at fault as Lexin for abandoning the unordained child. Still, Klara, who had been Queen at the time, forced her to send it to a human orphanage and forget it had ever happened. It discontinued whatever attraction Lexin and Arlo had with each other, but it was for the best. As Lexin would say, their love was not sewn into the tapestry. So it should have never been. Hades did not have to worry about damning Lexin's soul. God may have claimed his judgement, but he was not redeemed. That much I know.

Adelheid Hark

The trial went quickly and smoothly. I was worried at first when Hades won, what I believe was the trial, but it seemed more like a quarrel between him and Zeus. To my surprise, his only request was that I kill Lexin. I mentioned that I was already making him weak with poison. He told me that he knew and was looking forward to watching him die. I didn't know how to respond to that, so I just nodded uncomfortably and waited for them to send me back to Earth. Being sent back to Earth felt weird. Maybe because of the way I died. Ishalo had reluctantly shared that with me. I felt a tingly burning sensation and everything was black for a few moments and then I was back in the desert. It wasn't nearly as painful as the toxic Dordaglaje flames that consumed my body before I passed. When I got to the labs after my mothers coronation. I thought I would simply be airing it out. I was not expecting Radon 'the faithful Arspen warrior', as he introduced himself, to be waiting for me at the end of the hall as I entered. He said he was here for Lilian and he was glowing a bright green. It was very beautiful actually.

"Are you one of Lexin's failed experiments?" I asked, watching him radiate in the hallway of the labs.

"Oh no dear. I am one of the Arpsens successes. And this message is for Lilian from them," he smiled menacingly and began to glow brighter. "We hope you burn in the eternal flames, Tetachel! Just as you burned our people!"

"Sir! Lilian isn't even here!" I exclaimed. "Also, that looks like it's getting worse. Do you wanna maybe step outside?"

"It is too late. It is already over," he said as he began to laugh maniacally. I started to shield my eyes. The bright light grew so strong that I could no longer see his figure and my skin started to sizzle just the way it did that night when Cobalt intruded. Radon exploded, and suddenly the poison was everywhere. The walls were lined with flames of red and yellowish green. I was reduced to my knees and stopped myself from crashing to the ground with my hands out, sprawled on all fours. I started to choke, I could feel the poison traveling down my esophagus. It was an excruciating pain. I had never been burned before. It was impossible for me, but I would imagine it felt like that. I could barely keep my eyes open. The air was filled with a greenish yellow mist. I looked at my watch and pressed record.

"I don't know what happened!" I screamed through coughs and the crackling and popping of the labs burning around me. "The Arspens are coming for Lilian! I don't know how much longer I can—"

I suppose I sent the transmission. But after the poison fully consumed my vocal chords I had nothing left to say. I couldn't even cry. I don't know how long I laid there burning to death. I only know that after a while I didn't feel pain. And then it was over, like a fever dream. I landed in purgatory. I quarreled with my identities, I gained knowledge, had my trial and I'm back. It wasn't something you should just come back from, but there was no rule book for this and I didn't know what to do. So by nature, I went back to the labs. It looked different. They replaced the white walls and tiled floors with green walls of vine and dark wooden floors. When I turned the corner and passed Lexin's reestablished lab, I saw Mike down the hall. He stopped and stared for a moment before he ran up to me in joy.

"Hals?" he asked.

"Yes," I said. He grabbed me in his arms, and I returned his embrace. He let go and smiled at me for a second. I felt at ease, and then his smile faded.

"I wanted to say that Silas would be so happy to see you, but he likely won't," he said. I asked Mike what happened to the place as we walked to the cafeteria, and I finally got to eat after having no sense of smell, taste or awareness of hunger or thirst for months. He told me that after the coronation, the team returned to a completely destroyed lab. There wasn't even a body to bury, he had said. He told me about how CJ attempted to take over as captain, but the team truly fell apart without me. Just like Captain Hark said it would. Silas seldom left his room for a whole month. GG had decided to resign from the team and stopped going on missions. Lexin became sick and too weak to train us, so he mostly resided in his lab or room.

"After about a month or so, Lexin put Silas through the same procedure he did on you. He said he had to because they needed him for a mission. Apparently, CJ begged him not to do it, but I don't believe anything she says anymore," Mike said. My eyes widened.

"You know about the others?" I asked. Mike looked at me confused. "About what Lexin did to me?"

"I know that he messed with your brain. CJ told me he was going to. That's where he got the idea to get Silas out of his depression. I suppose it made things better for all of us, but I still feel guilty."

"Guilty about what?" I asked.

"Well it didn't help that you were gone. It hit Silas the hardest I think, but then GG and I... we hurt him," Mike said, looking down at the table.

"What happened?"

"I don't even want to say it. I'm so embarrassed," he said. I stuck out my hand and lifted his head by his chin, and looked him in the eyes.

"If I have to go searching for it myself, I will. Now, you've let the cat out of the bag, so you better just tell me. I'm not going to judge you, I promise." I said. I could tell he had changed since I had been gone. He had this air of wisdom and maturity around him, as opposed to how he was before when he was reckless and vulgar.

"In the past, I was... simply put—a man whore," he said. I looked at him, shocked at his choice of words. I would have never put it that boldly, but he wasn't wrong, so I didn't correct him. "I was proud of it, and no one ever stopped me because at the end of the day, I'm nobody. I had an addiction to it, to her. I chose her because I couldn't have you. She only took me because you had Silas, but now you don't and she does. And I... well, I had no one, and GG came out to Silas and he was already broken, so he neglected her. So, I was there, and she thought maybe she could be wrong."

"No... no, no," I whispered. Mike shook his head in shame and looked back down at the table. I knew what he had done. I didn't have to look into his mind or hear him say it. I just knew, considering his past and GG's innocence. Mike put his hands to his head and profusely shook as if he could hear the disappointment in my voice. I got up and went to sit next to him. I held him in my arms and squeezed him tight. "I'm not upset. It's not my business. You were all grieving. It's not your fault."

"But I just made things worse, and Silas hated me. I never realized that he considered me his brother. When he found out, he looked at me like I was participating in an act of insest, but I never saw GG that way. She was an orphan that lived in my home. She was fully raised. They both were. We just gave her shelter," Mike explained. He shook his head and looked at me. "I never even liked her like that. She was too easy and now I sound like a shallow douchebag."

"I understand. You made a mistake. I mean it's not like you. Well, what I mean to say is what you did, what you both did, was it consensual?" I asked. He looked away and nodded.

"Yes, of course, I would never... I mean, she practically begged me, but that doesn't matter," he said teary-eyed as he stared back down at the table.

"Mike don't... It's okay. Silas will forgive you," I said, rubbing his back as I tried to console him. He was sorry, I could tell. He felt terrible. I'm sure it made it worse that GG was still confused about who she was after the fact. He went through maturity and realized everything he did wrong in his youth was painful.

"I wish he would, but he doesn't remember anything of what we did. After he found out, he went into a fit of anger. Silas disowned GG and then he tried to kill me. CJ knocked him out and a month later, they took him to Lexin's lab. When he left the lab a week later, he had no memory of GG coming out or what we did. Worst of all, he called CJ his girlfriend and asked me for advice on how to propose. She told me that they fixed him. Obviously, they did much more than that."

I didn't even know what to say. I wasn't shocked about what had unfolded. Mike and GG's relationship was a surprise but mostly in character for Mike at the time. I could understand Silas lashing out and trying to kill Mike as I know he felt they were brothers the way I felt CJ was my sister. Could I blame her for doing what she thought was right to help Silas? Or should I assume that she only did it so she could have him for herself? I never invaded their mental privacy, but maybe I should start because she obviously did more than erase the tarnished memories he had of him and Mike's brotherhood or the image of his innocent, perfect little sister.

"Have you tried to fix him? Like with your healing powers?" I asked,

"I have, but, I can't seem to reach whatever mentally induced psychosis they put him in. Not by myself at least," he said as he looked at me. "But perhaps together, with your telepathy and my healing abilities, we could fix him."

"Maybe," I said. I smiled a little. Mike truly had changed. He knew bringing Silas back would make him remember again and put him back in a bad place with Silas, but he was ready to accept the consequences. "I just want to say, Mike. I see that you've really changed. The way you were described in that book that Hei... I wrote. I didn't write you to be the wise young gentlemen you seem to be now."

"You wrote what you knew; how you truly saw me," he said.

"But I was wrong. I've never seen you like this before. This attitude. The way you carry yourself now looks good on you," I said. We continued to look at each other. Face to face, eyes locked into each other's opposite gaze. "I like this Mike."

Then almost naturally, we kissed. But after a few seconds, Mike pulled away.

"You see! I have a problem! I keep hurting him," Mike said.

"What it sounds like to me is that Silas is with CJ now," I said.

"Ya! Against his will!" he screamed.

"Right. But I'm still alone, and so are you," I said.

"But we're still gonna bring him back right?" Mike asked.

"Yes, of course, but who says just because we fix Silas that things have to go back to the way they were before?" I asked.

"Because he loves you, and you're his," Mike said.

"I belong to no man but the very one that created me. I choose who I want. I have that power, because I'm a royal," I said. Mike shook his head in agreement and humbly apologized. "It's not just that, though. When I was at my mother's coronation, I had all those suitors chatting me up and chasing

me down, fighting for just a second of my time. Then, I finally realized that I could have anyone. I never allowed myself to
look past my own group of friends. I saw you, and I saw Silas
and you were… you were who you were at the time. And Silas
was there. Then we were here, and he was the only valid option.
It's not to say that I don't love him, but I also didn't have many
options either."

"And now, I'm the only valid option," Mike said, turning
away. I put my hand on his shoulder and guided him to turn
back towards me.

"That's not what I'm trying to say. I could've chosen any of
those suitors. I met with almost every Alpha Begavad male royal
this earth has to offer, and even still, I didn't want to be with any
of them. I thought I was bound to Silas, but maybe this is a sign
to show that I'm not," I said.

"Silas loves you," Mike said.

"And you don't?" I asked.

"Well of course. We all do. CJ covets your life. Lexin yearns
for your power. GG is the only one who isn't obsessed with you,
surprisingly," Mike said jokingly.

"I suppose I'm not her type," I said. Mike laughed. He
looked at me and smiled. "But you are… my type."

"Am I, though? Before you died, you never even considered
me your friend. Now, all of a sudden, you want to be my lover,"
Mike said. I sat speechlessly. I wasn't sure what he wanted me
to say. It was true that I had seen Mike differently before I died,
but I too realized a lot before then. I'm different now, and I have
been for a while. I have these personalities all pulling me in

different ways. "Well, why am I complaining? I've been waiting for the feeling to be mutual for years."

"It's late, and I haven't slept in five months. I'm exhausted, so I think I'm going to go to bed." I said, getting up from the table. Mike followed suit.

"Um, ya about that. CJ sort of took over your room," Mike said.

"Then I'll sleep in her room," I said.

"GG is in CJ's room now," Mike said. "And she's using her old room as a lab, so it doesn't even have a bed."

"Wow, a lot has really changed since I've been gone."

"You can sleep in my room. I will... I'll sleep here," Mike said, gesturing to the table.

"Mike, I'm not gonna let you sleep in the cafeteria," I said. I patted him on the back and headed towards the door. He followed beside me. "We're both mature adults. I think we can handle sharing a room for one night. Tomorrow, we will clean out GG's makeshift lab, and I will take my room back."

"Set everything back in order," Mike said. "Back to the way it was."

"Mostly," I said.

CJ (Claire-Joan) Johnson

Silas and I returned from our mission late. When I arrived at the cafeteria, I was shocked to see Adelheid sitting beside Mike and in front of GG, who was seated beside Silas, who was minding his own. When I approached the table, Adelheid looked up and analyzed my shock.

"I… I…" I stuttered.

"Can't believe I'm back, huh?" Adelheid asked. "Gosh, it's like you've seen a ghost, CJ."

"I'm so happy to see you. I kept your bed warm while you were… gone," I said cautiously.

"Unnecessary, but thank you," she said. She took a sip of her water without breaking her gaze. "I see you've changed a lot of things. I'll be setting everything back to normal now, as the captain."

"Uh… Well if you want the captaincy, you have to fight me for it," I said. Adelheid frowned, and Mike chuckled quietly while he shook his head.

"No, I don't. I'm Adelheid. I'm an Alpha Begavad and a royal. I named you as my successor in the case that I die. Which in all fairness, I did, but now I'm not so dead, which gives me all the right to take it back," she said.

"Yes. You're right. I apologize," I said, frazzled.

"Don't even worry about it girlfriend," she said sarcastically.

"So when did you get back, Adelheid?" Silas asked.

"Last night. I was exhausted, so I didn't have the energy to say hi, but Mike caught me up. Did you miss me?" she asked.

"Well, of course. It was different while you were gone," Silas said.

"Was it?" she asked. Silas nodded.

"Where did you sleep last night? I'm sure if Mike caught you up, then you must know that all the rooms were occupied," I said.

"I slept in Mike's room," she said.

"Oh," I said. She smiled at me again.

"Yes, well like you said, all the rooms were occupied, and Mike so generously offered me his since he was the only one here to greet me," she said, continuing to stare and smile towards me.

"Where did Mike sleep?" I asked.

"Who cares?" She remarked in an annoying tone. She rolled her eyes and then stood up. "Listen, Silas and Mike, I will need to see you in the practice room in ten minutes. GG, it's nice to see that you finally got your dream lab, but I need you to move it into Lexin's lab or the classroom. I don't really care. It just needs to be cleared so you can stay in your room again and CJ can have her room back. So obviously, CJ, while I conference with Mike and Silas, I'll need you to move out of my room. Maybe make yourself useful and help GG move her lab. I realize that Lexin is probably too old and weak to monitor y'all anymore, which is why I'm going to be taking care of our schedule from now on. Get to it."

She walked away, and I turned to Mike. I then waited until Silas and GG left to speak to Mike alone.

"What the hell did you say to her?" I asked Mike.

"I told her the truth, the whole truth and about this little simulation you're running. It's about to be over," Mike said.

"You realize that this doesn't benefit you right? If you turn Silas back, he will hate you again and not to mention your young lover," I said.

"GG is not my lover and you know that. And I know Silas is going to hate me, but unlike you, I'm ready to accept the consequences," he said.

"I saved you the last time. I won't do it again," I threatened.

"You won't have to," he said.

"I might. Especially when Silas finds out that you slept with his sister and his girlfriend," I said.

"You don't know anything, but I wonder how Silas will feel when he realizes that you've been using him as your boy toy."

"Silas loves me!"

"No he doesn't. He loves Heidi. He's always loved Heidi. You wanted what she had the same way I wanted what Silas had. We're two of the same, CJ. That's why we were attracted to each other in the first place. The only difference is that I have the strength to admit my faults and grow from them, while you cowardly take what you can get and cower in fear of the penalty. But hey, the apple doesn't fall far from the tree, now does it? I wonder what your dear boyfriend might think about his mother's heroic story and her mysterious death."

"You wouldn't. I told you that in confidence."

"I don't have to. Though I doubt Silas will blame you for your mother's mistakes, which left him and his sister orphaned. Honestly, I wouldn't be surprised. He'll already be heated with everything GG and I did. Though I'm sure he'll forgive us and take it as an opportunity to scold you, I mean, after everything you did."

"I don't get it. Heidi has you, and now you have her. That's what you want, right? Why bring back Silas just to break his heart furthermore?" I asked. Finally, Mike had nothing left to say. "Because that's what you'll do. He may get over the fact that GG is gay, he may even forgive you for what you did, but he will never forgive you for taking Heidi away from him. This way is better. He thinks he loves me, and if we keep it up, one day he actually will. You and I could both have what we want, but if you bring him back, you can never be with Heidi. Not even if she chooses you. Not while he's still living."

"What you don't understand is that I'm a good person who sincerely cares about their friend. I don't care if things don't work out with Heidi. Silas shouldn't have to live a lie, and if he truly loves Heidi, he would be able to let her go. However, in the end that will be her choice," he said. He then got up and left me to sit alone in the cafeteria. Adelheid was my best friend. My sister. My partner in crime. She left, and I got everything. Now, she's back and she's taking back my power. She's taking Silas, and now she has Mike wrapped around her finger. She probably hates me, but how could she blame me for taking what she left behind? I'm going to be alone forever, just the same way my mother subjected herself to a life of loneliness.

GG Pushman

I was packing my lab equipment into boxes with no help from CJ. I was halfway done when I heard a knock on my door.

"Forget it, CJ. I'm in a flow here," I said. I turned around and realized it was Adelheid standing by my door. She smiled at me and picked up an empty box by the door. "Oh. Sorry I thought you were CJ."

"No worries. I see she disobeyed my orders. Let me help you," she said.

"Sure. Have you spoken to Silas yet?" I asked.

"Didn't bother. I was going to, but Mike and I couldn't get through. He doesn't remember me. Now I know how it feels. Karma, I guess."

"Injustice is more the word I would use. I want Silas to accept me but not like this." I said, continuing to pack things away.

"I get it," she said, picking up a telescope and putting it neatly in the box. "I heard about you and Mike. Didn't think you'd tell anyone else."

"Thought you dying was a sign that I shouldn't, but then I just couldn't help wondering, what if."

"Well, what was it like?" she asked. I blushed and looked away. "Gosh, I can't believe Silas' little sister got some before I did."

"It was definitely something. Yet I felt more with you then I did with Mike, and it was just a kiss,"

I said, remembering our secret. "You're not still... ya know."

"Oh yes, honey. I follow all the rules and it seems like I'll be following them for a while longer."

"Well, there's always Mike," I said. She looked at me suspiciously. "But of course, you love my brother so that's obviously not going to happen. So I'm just saying he really likes you too. So if you could get over that, then... you know... Mike."

"Ya, I get it. He's just not into it. Dying makes you delusional for a minute. I shouldn't have made a move on him at all. Anyway, we're going to find a way to bring Silas back, and it wouldn't be right to break his heart twice."

"Right, my fault."

"No, it was a team effort. Seriously. We'll bring Silas back, and he'll forgive you. I'll get him to forgive you."

"If you could, that would be great. Just no mind games," I said. She nodded at me and gave me a sleazy smile.

"Hey… you wanna do some drugs?" She asked mischievously. We both giggled and I nodded. "Shall I?"

"No worries. I have some." I said as I took a spliff out of my pocket. "I've kind of been saving these ever since you left. I couldn't get high while you were gone because CJ refused to light them. Can you believe she's never done weed before?"

"She thinks she'll get addicted. She doesn't believe me when I tell her that just doesn't happen. Humans may get addicted, but most Begavads have enough willpower not to," she said, lighting the spliff with her finger.

"Not to mention that if you grow it from your hand, it may not be intoxicating at all," I added. She smiled at me and nodded.

"But that's the way we like it," she said, and we both laughed. There were four main things to do in the fortress: swim, train, hook up and get high. There really wasn't much else to do other than that. So once you got bored of one thing, you'd move on to the next. "You remembered what I taught you."

"Yep! Every earth Begavad can make weed, but it takes a good earth Begavad to make good weed," I said, reciting what she told me the first time she taught me how to make weed. We laughed and took a few puffs. It hadn't kicked in yet for me. I stared at Heidi to see if she felt it. As I was about to open my mouth to ask, she shook her head.

"Nothing yet, but I have a feeling it'll take effect soon. We might have to finish it," she said jokingly. There were a few moments of silence. Heidi looked me up and down a few times, and I felt as if she was struggling to ask me something. "Why did you come out to Silas while he was already down? I mean, you couldn't have thought that would be a good idea. We were taught a certain way. He was bound to reject you."

"That's not exactly what happened…" I said. I then reminded Heidi of the tapes. Lexin had us under constant surveillance. We used to go down in the sub-basement to watch the memories of our time at the labs. We always liked to think that was why he surveilled us, but honestly no one cared enough to ask. Before Silas slipped into his deep depression, I suggested we all go down to the sub-basement to watch tapes of Heidi to remember her. Silas agreed, and I thought I was a genius. I figured that it would make him feel better somehow. But the plan went horribly wrong when he found the tape that concealed my secret—the one Heidi had sworn to protect. "I didn't realize until it was already playing, and then I couldn't get him to turn it off. He was distraught, confused, angry and then he just snapped."

"What did he say?" she asked.

"A lot of things. Most of which I wish not to repeat. The point is, he saw what he perceived as a betrayal on my part and he disowned me. After that, he never came out of his room, not until the other incident." I wanted to cry, but I hated looking weak in front of Heidi, so I looked up at the ceiling and tried to calm myself down. Then I looked back at Heidi, who was giving me a sympathetic look. "Am I just fated to be a screw up?"

"No," she said simply.

"Silas seems to think so."

"He was grieving, but he didn't mean it."

"No, he did. You're right, it's what we were taught. We were taught to shun people like me."

Mike Larloff

I met Silas and Heidi in the practice room after warning CJ of what we were about to do. Heidi had Silas sitting on a chair and was waiting for me by the door.

"Do we have a plan?" I asked.

"We don't. I just thought you could do your thing, and I'd do mine," she said.

"Why do I need to be here?" Silas asked. Heidi shushed him and then placed her hand on his forehead.

"That won't work," Lexin said, standing in the doorway. "You are just a telepath, Adelheid. You could only remind him of his memories for a second. So, even if you had the ability of mind control, you still could not achieve what you are attempting."

"Then tell us how to fix him."

"And recreate a dysfunctional team? I do not think I will. You do realize that training you was my only job, and I have failed? So no, I will not help you," Lexin said. Adelheid growled and put an iced sword to his neck. "Go ahead, kill me. I have been waiting for you to do this for months."

She maintained the sword at his neck and the glare into his eyes. She shook her head and withdrew her sword.

"He's right. We can't fix him. Whatever he did was irreversible, at least by our hands. He'll have to break out of it himself, the way I did," she said. "All we can do is wait and pray."

Heidi shoved past Lexin, who gave me a sinister smile and wobbled away. I stood in front of Silas who had gotten up from his chair and turned to face me.

"That was really weird," he said.

"I know, buddy. I know."

"I wanted to show you something actually," he said as he pulled a ring from his back pocket and put it up to my face.

"Oh, please don't tell me you're going to marry her?" I asked disgustingly.

"I don't know. I thought I really wanted to, but now I'm not sure. The past few weeks with CJ have been a little weird. It's like I have these memories that seem questionable. I don't know. I sound crazy."

"No, no you don't. Why didn't you tell me about this before?" I asked.

"Because it sounds crazy. I just don't remember CJ the same way I used to, and when Adelheid came back, it was like... really weird, but I felt like she was more like CJ than CJ was like CJ. I don't know, man, it's crazy."

"Trust me, this is good."

"I looked at this ring. I got it from the Queen, but I could never quite work it out. The Queen gave me this ring to propose to CJ. That's what she told me, but it doesn't make much sense."

"Right, because that's a family heirloom, and Heidi is the Queen's daughter, not CJ."

"Right, and I asked her permission for the princess' hand, which is Heidi... well, this is why... I can't. No, let me start over. I'm confused," Silas went on like this for several minutes, re-explaining how he felt about CJ or Heidi. I tried to help, then he'd get confused again. Then out of nowhere, he looked me straight in the eyes, and his jaw dropped. Almost as if a light bulb had just gone off in his head. "Oh my gosh. I love Heidi."

I sighed with relief and sprung up from the ground.

"I will be right back, don't move."

"Wait, Mike! What's going on? What did you do to me?" he asked, confused. I nodded my head and gestured for him to stay. He plopped down on the chair again, and I ran down the hall. I heard the familiar giggling of Heidi in GG's room. I entered through a cloud of smoke and found Heidi and GG sitting on a desk, shocked to see me.

"How could you be high at a time like this?" I screamed. They stared at me for a few seconds as if I was a stranger and then burst into hysterical laughter.

"Do you want some?" Heidi asked between giggles.

"No!... uh... well... maybe later, but right now you should come with me!" I said, snatching Heidi by the arm and dragging her back to Silas.

"What the hell, Mike!" she yelled.

"He remembers! He remembers!" I said happily.

"What did you do?" she asked.

"Nothing, he did it on his own," I said as we approached the training room.

"So quick? How?" she asked.

"Does it matter?" I asked. Silas met eyes with Heidi and it was like in an instant it all clicked. We went into the room and Heidi kneeled down in front of him. He looked at the ring and at Heidi. He smiled, noticed me, and looked disappointed. That's how I knew for sure, that he remembered. CJ came to the door and asked what was going on. Silas looked at her and became visibly angry.

Silas Pushman

It was like I had seen my life flash before my eyes. At first, I was confused, rambling the same words over and over to Mike, and then everything became clear. I saw CJ standing in the doorway. I formed into ice and drew my sword then charged for CJ. She jumped back and burst into flames. She shot me with an arrow that went right through my shoulder, but it didn't stop me from striking her with my sword. CJ fell to the ground, and just as I was about to finish the job, Heidi came between us.

"Stop!" Heidi screamed. She looked at me, CJ, and then me again. Finally, CJ got up and stood back cautiously. "Silas, I know that you're mad. I get it, but this is not the way."

"You're mad at me? Only me? I'm not the one who slept with your sister!" she shouted.

"CJ, please!" Heidi begged.

"She messed with my head. I almost... I almost did things I would have regretted for the rest of my life because I thought she was you. If we were in the fortress this is how she would be punished," I said, as I tried to move around Heidi. She blocked me again, giving me a stern look this time and pushing me back with her hands in flames.

"Lexin did that to you!" CJ yelled.

"But you didn't stop him," I said.

"Neither did they, and I'm sure you remember full well what they did to you," she said. I looked at Mike and grunted.

"Doesn't even compare," I said. "You helped him mess with my brain! You held me down!"

"Silas, put down your sword! CJ, cool down!" Heidi yelled to us.

"Too bad you won't get the chance to kill me today," CJ said.

"That's fine. I'll get you in your sleep."

"I'd like to see you try."

"I don't!" Heidi said, breaking up our quarrel. I was so upset I barely even realized she was still there. She looked at me concerningly and then turned to CJ. "CJ, you have to leave."

"For how long?" CJ asked.

"Forever. I'm banishing you," Heidi said. "You broke my trust. You manipulated and experimented on one of our own, so you can't be here anymore. Silas is right. If this was the fortress, you would be killed. I don't want to do that. So if you leave, I'll say that you got away, and if you don't, well, I'm not going to protect you here."

CJ formed back to her skin, and so did I.

"And what of Lexin? Will he also be banished for his part?" she asked.

"Lexin is slowly but surely dying. He's paying for his crimes," Heidi exclaimed.

"Silas, I'm sorry," CJ said.

"Go to hell CJ," I said angrily.

"Just leave before I let him kill you," Heidi said. CJ turned away and left. I was left in the room with Heidi by my side and Mike across the room. He was standing back cautiously. I put out my hand.

"I don't suppose I'm next?" he asked. He took my hand and I shook it.

"We're cool. I just can't look you in the eyes for a few days, that's all," I said.

"You have to know that I'm sorry. You have to know that," Mike said.

"I know. I forgive you," I said.

"Alright, it's just… you're freezing my hand, that's all. Makes me feel as though you are still very upset," he said. I looked down, and I was freezing his hand. I seemed to be a little upset subconsciously, but I was sure that would pass, so I released him. "I deserved that."

Adelheid Hark

Silas had come back on his own. I was glad it didn't take long, as I was already planning a trip to Mars and I didn't want to leave him in that state. My mother and I were going to sign a peace treaty on behalf of the Earthly Begavad, and we had to go over the contract. It would take many days, and I was hoping to get her advice about my situation. I was sure she'd tell me to follow my heart, but I knew she wanted me to marry Silas. He was good to me. However, my mom didn't know how Mike had changed. And I was changing, and a part of me had outgrown Silas. I didn't know what I was going to tell him, but I knew that afterward, we would need space.

I invited Silas to my room to talk. However, we didn't get to it right away. He was so happy to see me, and I couldn't resist him either. When things cooled down, we sat on my bed in silence for a while. "Thank you for banishing CJ," he said.

"Of course. She hurt you and me, everyone really," I said.

"I didn't do anything with her," he said. I looked at him, reluctant to tell him the truth.

"I know, but it doesn't matter," I said. He pulled out a ring from his back pocket, and I looked away. "I can't accept that, Silas."

"But you can. It's your family heirloom," he said. I looked back at it. It was. I suppose my mother gave it to him.

"No, I can't because I'm not going to marry you," I said. Silas threw the ring in my lap.

"Just take it Adelheid. Take it and give it to Mike then," he snarled.

"I'm not going to marry Mike. I'm not going to marry any-one right now," I gently replied. "I need some time alone."

"You're breaking up with me for Mike now?" he asked.

"Are you even listening? This is not about him," I said.

"I wasn't able to be myself when Lexin messed with my head, but I do remember everything said, and I know that you were with him the night you returned. It's not fair that you gave up on me and instantly latched onto him," he said. He got off of my bed and walked up to the wall, turning his back towards me.

"I haven't... I didn't. I am different now, and I need to figure out who I am," I said.

"You don't know who you are, huh? Seems like you're not alone. Does Mike's healing abilities also include conversion therapy because it seems like that's what he's being used for," he said. Silas turned to face me, and I got out of bed to confront him.

"Don't say that. You don't even know what I'm going through," I said forcefully.

"What you're going through?" he asked.

"Yes! Because I just died, and returned to all these changes. You were with CJ, and I know that's not your fault, but it's not mine either. Mike was there, and he was different. He helped me realize that I went for the easiest catch!"

"Did you just call me easy?"

"No, kind of… Not really. The point is, I am different now. The reality shift gave me clarity you couldn't even begin to understand and then dying was traumatic," I said, holding back my urge to strangle him. I sighed as I tried to calm down. "I'm leaving tonight for Mars. My mother and I are going to sign a peace treaty on behalf of the Earthly Begavad with the Martian council. We should both take this time to reflect and figure out what we want. I do love you, but I need to figure myself out before I give any more of myself to you."

"Fine," he reluctantly replied.

"Try to make up with your sister. She misses you," I said, putting my hand on his shoulder. He moved it away, nodded and left. It didn't go as bad as I thought it would. I knew it would be difficult to rekindle anything we had once I returned, but I had to be sure Silas was who I wanted. Most of all, I had to be sure that I was ready to accept my fate.

Now, I know what you must be thinking, this is no way to end a story. Questions left unanswered, hearts broken, families

destroyed, psychological trauma undealt with and our story's favourite couple broken apart! How can it end now when so many
things have yet to be uncovered? Well, let's remember why I
started to recount this story in the first place. It was never for
you. It was for me, so that I may know the truth and figure out
how to prosecute the guilty. Well, lucky for you, I haven't come
to a conclusion yet. Not even close. This story is not over. In fact,
it is just the beginning.

INDEX

Begavad - Swedish for *gifted*: A Begavad is an extraordinary immortal being who has the ability to embody and manipulate the four elements, air, earth, fire and water. When Begavads take their elemental form it allows them to become invincible and regenerate if they are injured, from a scratch to a decapitation.

Alpha Begavad: A Begavad who possesses all four elements, usually direct relation with the first five Begavad

Pentaelkay: A Begavad who possesses more than one element

Elemente: A Begavad who possesses one element

Dordaglaje - derivative of döda glädjen is Swedish for *kill joy*: A poisonous flower made from pure evil, death, hate and treachery, naturally grown in the garden of Hecate, the only substance that can kill a Begavad. Alpha's are immune to the gas but not to the liquid or solid if it impales them or enters their bloodstream.

Dodaroite - derivative of döda rot is Swedish for *kill root*: The Martian word for Dordaglaje

Mordare - Swedish for *killer*: A briefly mentioned prophecy.

CPSIA information can be obtained
at www.ICGtesting.com
Printed in the USA
BVHW072304080223
658188BV00004B/80